THE
COURAGE
TEST

THE
COURAGE
TEST

JAMES PRELLER

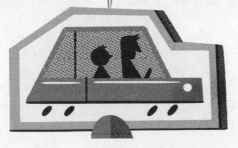

FEIWEL AND FRIENDS
NEW YORK

A FEIWEL AND FRIENDS BOOK
An Imprint of Macmillan

THE COURAGE TEST. Copyright © 2016 by James Preller.
All rights reserved. Printed in the United States of America by R. R. Donnelly & Sons
Company, Harrisonburg, Virginia. For information, address Feiwel and Friends,
175 Fifth Avenue, New York, N.Y. 10010.

Our books may be purchased in bulk for promotional, educational,
or business use. Please contact your local bookseller or the Macmillan
Corporate and Premium Sales Department at (800) 221-7945 ext. 5442
or by e-mail at MacmillanSpecialMarkets@macmillan.com.

Library of Congress Control Number: 2016937798

ISBN 978-1-250-09391-2 (hardcover) / ISBN 978-1-250-09392-9 (ebook)

Book design by April Ward

Feiwel and Friends logo designed by Filomena Tuosto

First Edition—2016

1 3 5 7 9 10 8 6 4 2

mackids.com

This book is dedicated to my oldest son, Nick, who has become my faithful first reader. Nick helped me think through parts of this book and has taught me—across the years—many lessons about true courage.

And also, a special shout-out to my friend Cyndi, a wise survivor who has navigated those difficult conversations with her children. She, too, has shined a light upon the courageous path.

—J.P.

CONTENTS

We shall not cease from exploration

And the end of all our exploring

Will be to arrive where we started

And know the place for the first time.

—T. S. ELIOT, *FOUR QUARTETS*

MY NAME IS WILLIAM MERIWETHER MILLER.
I was named after the explorers William Clark and Meriwether Lewis. It was my dad's idea. So I guess this trip was inevitable, like homework and awkward school dances. He's dragging me down the old trail.

It's the last thing in the world I want to do.

We were now

about to penetrate

a country at least two thousand miles

in width, on which

the foot of civilized man

had never trodden.

—MERIWETHER LEWIS

CHAPTER ONE
OFF THE MAP

My mother pushes me out the door, and I don't know why.

"I don't want to go," I tell her.

"I know," she says.

"But why now?" I ask again. "All-Stars starts this week. I don't want to miss it."

"We've been over this," she says.

She might as well say what every parent resorts to when they run out of good answers: *Because I said so.* There's no explanation, no more discussion. It's time for me to go.

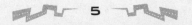

I feel ridiculously, stupidly, helplessly annoyed, and there's nothing I can do about it. I see in that instant my mother is getting old. Stray gray hairs, wrinkles around the down-turned corners of her mouth. She looks tired and thin, sick of arguing with me. I carry a fully loaded metal-frame backpack on my shoulders and a smaller gym bag in my right hand—stuff for the long drive, all my technology's in there. I don't want to go, but I can't stand here forever. So come on, Mom, let's do this.

"You'll have fun," she says. "It's good for you and your father to spend time together."

"Please, Mom."

"He's the only father you've got," she says.

I give her nothing in return. Not a nod. I'm not even listening. I turn my back to her.

"Bye," she says, and adds, "I love you, Will."

I walk away like I don't hear.

"Will?"

I raise my hand in good-bye without looking back.

My father waits in the car. He steps out as I

approach. I nod to him, hey. None of this is my idea. I have no say, no choice. I refuse to be happy about it. I'm not going to make this easy.

"Here, um, let me help you with that." He reaches to take my backpack.

"No, I got it," I say, leaning away.

"Oh, okay, sure," he says.

He stands there, not knowing what to do.

"Are you going to pop the trunk?" I ask. Because: obviously.

Flustered, my father moves to the driver's side door. He fumbles in the front pocket of his water-resistant khakis, drops the keys on the road, stoops to the ground. I glance sideways, slyly, to check how this is playing from the front window. But my mother is no longer watching.

She's gone.

"Ready?" my father asks. His body is half turned in inquiry, one hand on the steering wheel, the right gripping the ignition key.

A question with no true answer.

I don't have a choice. *So, sure, Dad*, I shrug, *I'm ready*. But the truth is I'm not. He knows it, too, yet asks anyway. And away we roll.

It is awkward all around.

This is the man who moved out of the old house fifteen months ago. He started a shiny new life— soon featuring a new girlfriend—while my mother and I got stuck rebuilding the old one.

As the car slides forward, I spy my friend Yoenis on the sidewalk. Tall and dark and slender, he juggles a soccer ball on his foot, *tap-tap*, *tap* and *pop*, and he snatches the ball between his hands. A bright smile sunbeams across his face. He's a guy who can do anything he wants. Yoenis glimpses me through the car window, and his smile drops. He waggles a finger skyward. His head shakes. I don't know what it means. Is he pointing to the sun, the sky? Is he gesturing to God above? Or is he just saying, no, don't go, you'll miss everything.

I wonder if he knows something I don't know?

Thwap, thwap, thwap.

I am sprawled, unbuckled, in the backseat—my

choice, not his, more legroom—playing catch by myself. A glove on my right hand, a baseball in my left. Yeah, I'm a southpaw from Minneapolis. I'm making a point. He can drag me away from the game and All-Stars and from all my friends. But he can't make me forget it—and I won't let him, either.

I don't forgive easily.

"Meri, please," he says, "not in the car. It's a distraction when I'm driving."

There is a pause now, a moment that stretches out for a mile or so as the car zooms past the windblown grasses of the prairie landscape. West, west. And then I start up again.

Thwap, thwap, thwap.

When he checks the rearview mirror, he can see my grin.

"And don't call me Meri," I say. "Please, *Bruce*, it's annoying."

I've never called my father Bruce before, and I watch as his eyeballs register the disrespect. Blinking, thinking, not responding.

We are headed to a place near Bismarck, North Dakota, where I guess there's a museum or fort or old

Indian village or something. Dad says I'm going to love it. But I think, *Not if I can help it.*

As if reading my mind, my father says, "You can't stay angry the entire trip."

Want to bet?

He passes back a bag of Doritos. I agree to eat them, crunching loudly on the orangey goodness. Being a jerk is exhausting. My father knows how to inch over to my good side. It's through an extra-large bag of Doritos.

To pass the time, my father tells fifty miles of cringeworthy jokes. Each one is worse than the next. He's trying really hard—I can see that—but still. This is making my ears bleed. Then he says, "I read this one in a magazine. Let me see if I can remember it."

He says this before every single joke he tells. "Let me see . . ."

I'm slumped in the backseat, barely listening. This is going to be a long, long ride.

"Oh, yeah, okay," he says, snapping his fingers.

"A man and a woman are watching the news on television when the announcer says that six Brazilian men died in a car accident. Upon hearing this, the woman starts sobbing hysterically. She can't stop. 'It's sad, honey,' the man finally says, 'but accidents happen.' After a minute, still sobbing, she asks, 'How many is a Brazilian?'"

Before I can help it, a small laugh escapes my lips. I hate it when my father says something funny when I'm trying like crazy to stay mad at him. He's not making this easy.

Where in the world are we going?

Good question.

Right now we're on a highway headed west toward North Dakota. My father says our trip really begins there, at Fort Mandan, where the explorers Lewis and Clark and the entire Corps of Discovery hunkered down for the winter of 1804–1805. After that, they went into the unknown.

Uncharted territory.

Disconnected from the so-called civilized world.

My father is a college professor at the University of Minnesota in Minneapolis. He's obsessed with American history. For the past ten years, or nearly my entire life on the planet, he's been trying to write a book about the Lewis and Clark expedition. He even has a title, *Off the Map*, which I think is not half bad. Whenever I ask him how much he's written, he shrugs and looks away. He says he's been "focusing on the research end of the enterprise," whatever that means.

He has a girlfriend now. So maybe that's part of it. A blond-haired lady named Susan. She's okay, I guess, for someone I almost hate. She tries too hard and smells like apricots. Every time I'm over there, Susan wants to cook my favorite meals, play board games, "enjoy together time."

Who plays board games anymore?

She's always right in my face, asking, "So how are YOU today?"

How is anybody supposed to answer that? I say, "Fine," and my father gets mad at me for not answering politely. Nothing I do or say is good enough. I'm supposed to be a "new and improved" version of my old self. But really, I just want to go into my room and shut the door.

My dad is always asking me to give Susan a chance. I don't know how to answer him, exactly. It feels like a pop quiz every time I go over there, and I keep flunking it. I'm trying to be myself. Sorry that's not good enough anymore.

When my parents got divorced, it came as a big surprise to me, because what kid ever thinks about that stuff? Parents are just *there*, like a mountain or a river. A natural fact. You don't question it. Then one still-wintery day in March they sat me down for a talk. When they finished, they solemnly asked if I had any questions. I said, "Can I go Yoenis's house? He got the new FIFA game."

They were like, "What?"

I don't know. What was I supposed to say? What did it matter anyway?

I didn't even cry until a week later. And even then, hardly at all.

Spilt milk, you know.

The main thing as far as I was concerned was that

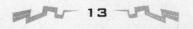

I could stay with my mom. At least most of the time. My father is okay, but he's one of those not-really-there types. It's hard to describe. His mind drifts. He's not into sports like I am. He works too much, reads too much. And now there's the irritating girlfriend added to the mix.

To be brutally honest, I don't think he actually wants me around. My mom is the one who has always taken care of me. She's a big Twins fan, and we always shared stuff like that, eating ice cream and watching the games on television. She actually stands up and yells at the TV sometimes. It's pretty funny. I remember once a reliever gave up a walk-off, three-run homer and she threw an entire bowl of popcorn at the screen. *Ha*, too funny. Even though they lost, it was worth it, just to see her go a little crazy like that. Popcorn everywhere! I think that's what makes a true fan of a team. You have to scream a little bit. My mom says that if the Twins don't rip your heart out every once in a while, then you just don't love 'em enough.

I sometimes go to my father's apartment for

weekends. It's not a regular thing, maybe once a month. He gets super busy. We go to Angela's restaurant most Wednesdays; they make the most excellent chicken Parmesan. I could eat that stuff forever. It's totally delicious—I order it every time. Sometimes I wonder if I could only eat one food in the world for the rest of my life, what food would that be. And I always end up saying, "Angela's chicken Parm!"

Yoenis says he'd pick Slim Jims. You know, the meat-like, stick-shaped, processed-food substance. Tasty, sure, but I think it would be a big mistake. After about four years of nothing but Slim Jims, I told Yoenis, a guy might lose his mind.

So it came as a big surprise when my split-up parents suddenly decided that I was going away with my father, without the dreaded Susan, on this trip to nowhere along the Lewis and Clark Trail. I was like, "Excuse me?" And then I was like, "Oh, no I'm not."

But here I am.

I mean, rewind. It's not *the trip* that I'm mad about. We're going to do a lot of cool things, camping and rafting and hiking, stuff I haven't done since

Boy Scouts. So all of that is fine. Better than fine. It's the timing. I made All-Stars this year. Coach says it's a commitment. You have to make every practice. You can't miss games. That's never been a problem for me in the past. I love All-Stars. But this year, out of the blue, my parents made other plans. Thanks for nothing.

I've been in the car for three hours now. I have to pee, but I'm not going to be the first one to say so. He checks, and I grumble back, "I'm fine."

I can't help but wonder what's going on here. I mean, why is it suddenly a big deal that I go on this trip? This isn't normal for my broken family. Suddenly my father wants "together" time? Pretty strange. So, yeah, what's up with that?

Now about Lewis and Clark: I'm not Joe Expert on the subject, but my father actually might be, so I have the basic plot. You can't hang around my father for long without him going off on his favorite topic. That's why Thomas Edison invented headphones. Or was that Dr. Dre? Never mind! I'm zoning out here in the backseat.

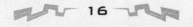

MY SUMMER ASSIGNMENT
by William Miller

This summer I went on a road trip with my father. We followed parts of the Lewis and Clark Trail. At first, I thought it was the most boring idea in the world. I'd rather go to Disney World. Well, buckle up, here comes the part where I tell you about it and you give me an A for effort.

When Thomas Jefferson was president, a lot of North America was unexplored. No white American had ever seen huge parts of it. The maps back then had all these details about the country out east where everybody lived—the names of towns and rivers and mountains—but beyond, like, west of the Mississippi River, the maps were basically blank. Just big, empty white spaces, not filled in at all, like an outline drawing in a coloring book you find on the shelf of the dentist's office. Way off to the left of the map it would be like, "Oh, and that's the Pacific Ocean somewhere out here we pretty much think!" They color in that part blue.

After the Louisiana Purchase in 1803, the United States government realized they owned all this land they didn't know anything about. Basically, Jefferson told Meriwether Lewis, "Dude, look, you have to go out there and check it out." Jefferson hoped that Lewis could find a water route across North America all the way to the Pacific Ocean. The Great Northwest Passage! That would be good for trade and— ca-ching!—profits. Jefferson thought there might even be mastodons wandering around, huge ground sloths, mountains made of salt, and Indian tribes that spoke Welsh. They really had no idea. True fact! Lewis realized it was a huge job, so he teamed up with his old army pal William Clark. They hired about thirty rugged, adventurous guys and set out looking for the heart of America. The plan was to start in St. Louis and go north up the Missouri River and try to float all the way to the ocean.

Oh, and by the way, there might be "hostile Indians" out there, so they brought guns, ammunition, and a lot of trinkets to give away. They figured the Indians were into bling. Beads and mirrors and stuff. What the Native people really needed were guns, because to them guns meant safety, and guns meant power. Their world was becoming a dangerous place. Jefferson instructed Lewis to tell the Indians they had a brand-new, powerful father—the president of the United States. Nobody was too sure how that news would go over with the Indians.

What a mess!

We wake up in a Budget Inn in Bismarck, North Dakota. We rolled in last night in the dark after driving more than 425 miles, 94 West practically all the way. My eyeballs burned with boredom and screen haze.

My dad did a bunch of yoga on the hotel room floor when I was trying to watch TV. He says I should try it, too, but I'm like, "Yeah, not really."

This place doesn't even have a pool.

My mother forgot to pack my toothbrush. Two weeks without one might be harsh.

And, even worse, my father snores like a walrus, which is just terrific.

He explains that yesterday's endless drive was a "necessary evil" and that the real adventure begins today. It's funny. He's actually excited in a way that's not normal for grown-ups. I also think he's trying extra hard to get on my good side because when he asked about breakfast he mentioned that there's a Denny's not far from here.

He knows I could live at Denny's. I mean, literally, I could live there. If I was in a booth, of course. I'd kick out my legs and lie back for a little snooze until the next glorious meal. Are they fast at Denny's? Good question. Yes, they are fast. You say your order out loud, and literally before you reach the end of the sentence there it is, steaming hot on the table in front of you. How is that possible? No one knows. Pancakes, bacon, scrambled eggs, and toast. The Grand Slam, partner!

During breakfast, my father talks about our trip. "Will, I know this got suddenly dropped on you and

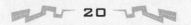

I'm sorry for that"—he looks at me over his western omelet, and his apology seems real—"but I need you with me right now."

I keep eating. What can I say? These pancakes are delicious. There's nothing remotely healthy about them. It's just pure, fluffy deliciousness. When my mom makes pancakes, she's always trying to sneak in oat bran or spinach leaves or protein powders or other "healthful" ingredients. You don't get that at Denny's. So I'm shoveling food into my face super happily. *Glomb, glomb, glomb.* Still, I'm listening, and I don't completely get what's going on.

He needs me? Since when?

"What do you mean?" I ask.

My father leans back, stares at the ceiling for long minutes. He's a college professor, so he's used to thinking that everything he says is a huge, big deal. He builds a lot of dramatic pauses into everyday conversations.

Then he surprises me.

"You know I've been working on my book for the past thirteen years," he says.

Thirteen? It was worse than I thought.

"I made the classic mistake: I kept researching long after I needed to start writing. Now I feel like I know too much, like"—he looks up again, as if the words were written on the ceiling—"like I'm wandering around inside a warehouse filled with facts."

Okay, sure. I imagine the last scene from *Raiders of the Lost Ark*. All those rows and rows of boxes.

"And you think I can help," I say. "Because I don't know anything."

"Exactly," my father says, smiling with his big horse teeth and sunken cheeks.

At least he's honest.

"When Meriwether Lewis came to these lands, he had no idea what he'd find. Sure, there were stories and rumors and wild guesses, but that was it. He had never seen a prairie dog before, Will. He had no idea they even existed. Or a magpie. Or a coyote! Or a pronghorn antelope! Lewis and his men were seeing a new world for the first time. I am hoping," my father says, and now he pushes his plate away, signaling for the bill from our helmet-haired server, Loretta, "I mean, I am *asking* if you'll help be my eyes."

I think it over.

I can't help but wonder if I'm missing something, but I don't ask. I get a sense that he's holding back. Or maybe he's just lying to me. There must be another reason for this weird vacation, but for the moment I can't figure it out. All I say is, "Next time, can I order bacon on the side?"

"All you want," he says, smiling wide.

He thinks I believe him.

My dad pulls over, says over his shoulder: "Won't be a sec, don't disappear on me," and hurries into a store.

I sit in the passenger seat and don't disappear.

Not really an option.

There's always that debate about which superpower you'd rather have, flight or invisibility. That's an easy one for me. I'd gladly vanish into thin air.

On the sidewalk, I see a black-haired teenage girl in a bulky blue flannel and dark pants. She's got a heavy, colorful cloth bag slung over her shoulder, and she's holding a thick rope. Attached to the rope is one of the biggest dogs I've ever seen. A Newfoundland, I'm pretty sure; it looks like a small domesticated bear. The girl is walking in my direction, so I watch her coming like a sunrise. Her long hair has been parted in the middle, but not expertly. Some falls across her face, which is too bad, because it's a good, pumpkin-shaped face with wide cheekbones and brown skin. The dog doesn't strain or pull, just matches her stride for stride.

As they reach the side of the car, the dog stiffens and stops, looks at me through the window. The girl tilts her head down and follows the dog's gaze to meet my eyes. That's how we first meet. She glances at invisible me, looks through me as if through a window in that briefest instant. There is no expression on her face, not even surprise, as if nothing in this world could surprise her. Her eyes are round and brown. She says something to the dog in Spanish, a soft, clear voice: *No es nada*, and gives a tug. In a graceful movement—the shift of a hip and the dip of a shoulder—she slips the strap closer to her neck and trudges on up the road.

A moment later, I'm startled when my father opens the car door, breaking the enchantment.

My father and I didn't start at the beginning. We didn't have time to retrace the whole entire Lewis and Clark Trail. The expedition officially began in May 1804, out of St. Louis and up the Missouri River, against the current. They traveled by a specially built, fifty-five-foot-long keelboat. It had a mast and sail for when the wind was right, but most days the men had to pull on oars or get out of the keelboat, walk on shore, and haul the heavy, awkward barge across shallow sections by thick ropes. It was brutal, backbreaking labor. They also traveled with two pirogues, which were like big rowboats. Some days they made twenty miles. Other days, far less. The farther north, the deeper the group traveled into the untamed American landscape—buffalo country and Indian territory and the great grasslands—where they encountered the Otos, the Arikara, and the Sioux. There were some awkward, tense meetings. Where the Missouri turned west, Lewis and Clark decided to winter near the friendly, curious Mandan and Hidatsa tribes. They built a fort and hunkered down. It was early November, and the frozen months were coming down hard. They had traveled more than 1,500 miles—every inch of it upstream, the current pushing relentlessly against them. But in many ways, their journey, like ours, had just begun.

He hands me a white paper bag. "A small gift," he says, "for our journey."

Inside there's a marbled composition notebook and a halfway-decent pen. I look at my father, wondering what this is all about.

"It's a journal," he said. "I want you to—"

"Dad, no," I interrupt. "We're on vacation. I'm not keeping a diary."

He raises his hands, the way a rancher might calm an agitated stallion. "You don't *have* to write anything, Will," he says. "I just want you to have it in case you change your mind. Recording what you see and feel, that's a big part of any trip. Journals were an integral aspect of the original expedition. Lewis was actually a terrific writer. Clark, too. Several of the other guys wrote books about their adventures."

He names names: Gass and Ordway and more.

"In some ways," my father says, "the journals were the greatest legacy of the expedition. They saw things that had never before been seen by white men. Their journals became documents. Artifacts. Records. Without the writing, the trip wouldn't have mattered half as much."

His cheeks grow flushed; he's waving his hands excitedly, like he's been bitten by red ants. I tuck the notebook and pen into my gym bag in the backseat. He watches this, but says nothing.

"You know what's interesting?" my father asks. He opens the glove compartment, mutters absently. It's stuffed with papers and junk. I don't ask him what's interesting, because I have a feeling he's going to tell me anyway.

He says, while still searching through the glove

compartment, "Lewis had to plan for a two-year-plus trip when he had no idea exactly where he was going or what, or even who, he would encounter. It was an ultimate, impossible grocery list. For months, he made list after list. Adding new items, scratching things off. He had to think of everything. They brought a hundred ninety-three pounds of practically inedible soup! Guns, ammunition, tobacco, knives, sewing needles, gifts for the Indians, tents, shirts, blankets, shoes, whiskey, scissors, rope—and on and on."

"That's a lot of stuff," I say, because at this point somebody besides my father has to say something. If I knew how to whistle, this would have been the perfect spot for it. A musical "big wow" from my lips. I don't feel like absorbing a life lesson right now. So I imagine that I have a shield made of vibranium like Captain America's—anything of educational value that my father says bounces right off.

"And along the way," my dad drones on, "they ran out of nearly everything." He ticks them off on his manic fingers. "They ran out of booze, coffee, tobacco—even gifts for the Indians, which would have been very useful to have by the time they met the Blackfeet, believe me. They ran out of everything except for paper and ink! That's how important it was to write, Will. It wouldn't have been the same remarkable, astonishing, courageous trip if they hadn't written about it."

He pauses, and says almost to himself, "Without the words, it would almost have been useless."

I hear him. I do. Some of his words actually get through my superhero defenses. I just don't want to let him turn my vacation into homework, but that's what teachers do. Today's next assignment: things I did on my summer vacation. So I nod my head and fake a smile.

I offer this crumb: "If this trip ever gets interesting, maybe I'll give it a try."

"Oh, no worries about that," he tells me. "The whole world is interesting, William, if you look at it the right way."

"I saw a girl," I disclose, to my surprise.

"Oh?"

"She had a huge black dog."

Now it's his turn to not listen. He's plugging an address into the GPS, which he finally located tucked under the driver's seat. And I'm left remembering that girl walking down the street, like a melody in my ear. Somehow I know that I will see her again.

In the museum gift shop, I grab a random postcard. It has a photo of the fake fort on front. One of these days I'm going to get stamps and mail this sucker.

The soldiers on the expedition built a fort here, but it's long gone. So the tourist board built an exact replica. Whatever! The tour guide told us it got as cold as 45 degrees <u>below zero</u> that winter. <u>Brrrrr, chilly.</u> The soldiers almost ran out of food, but fortunately the people of the Mandan tribe were super friendly. They had corn to spare! Otherwise those guys might have starved. We'd all be like, Lewis and Clark? Nope, never heard of 'em. Ha!

After my father left us, we had some rough times. I guess I acted creepy, but what can I say? I *felt* creepy. And it wasn't an act! I didn't try to get into trouble at school, trouble just found me. Stupid stuff, mostly, like falling off chairs, being disrespectful to elders, running when I should walk. My big crime? I had a bad attitude. I got to know the principal's office pretty well. The chairs are comfortable, I'll say that. It always got a gigantic reaction from my college-professor father—he went bananas, claimed I was ruining my life, and so on and so on. Maybe I enjoyed torturing him a little bit. My mother didn't react half as much, claiming that she refused to water the weeds.

There was a time, right when it was first happening, when it *hurt* to look at my father's face. I mean, it *physically hurt*. I'd want to heave. Maybe I'd done it for too long, watched him slurp cereal for too many years, blow his nose with the same fury, pick his nasty toenails. I mostly got tired of his face. His eyebrows don't match for starters, and one eye, the right one, is slightly square. His earlobes don't hang loose— he's got the attached kind that grow directly into his neck. When I look in the mirror, I see those same defects in me. It's discouraging. How am I ever going to meet a girl with this mug? My father sometimes runs his tongue across his giant teeth and emits a high-pitched sucking noise. It sounds like the mating call of a swamp toad.

He can't throw a ball. How is that even possible, I wonder, for a man—an ex-boy, supposedly—to be unable to throw a ball? You just grip the thing, rear back, and let 'er go. But for my father, somehow the elbow gets involved and everything collapses like a folding chair. It's hard to explain. Imagine a pink flamingo trying to throw a curveball, and that's pretty much my dad. He steps spastically forward on the wrong foot—his right, insanely!—no matter how many times I've tried to explain it. Hey, numbnuts, you step with the opposite foot! A person having a catch with my father literally has no idea where the ball will go. It could be seriously anywhere.

One thing my father can do is hike—quickly, jerkily, tirelessly—neck extended, head jutting out, elbows flapping, chest thrust forward. It looks like he's about to fall with a face-plant to the ground. But he never does. He just keeps motoring along. Effective, but definitely not athletic. Dad can walk a blue streak. When he thinks no one is watching, he digs around inside his nose with a thumb. No, not digs; he excavates, like he's an archaeologist searching for King Tut's cousin's tomb—buried inside his actual nose! His socks are always wrong, his shirts never match his pants, and don't get me started on the fanny pack! Who even wears fanny packs anymore? Nobody! Except for my dad, who swears by them.

On the positive side (to be fair and balanced), he's like a mild, G-rated version of the honey badger. My father doesn't care what anybody thinks. Craziest of all, most of that stuff doesn't bother me anymore. A year ago it made me crazy. Now it's just . . . typical Dad, doing what he does. I guess I'm stuck with him.

I do wish he could throw a ball, though. That might have been nice.

Once again, annoyingly, we are driving forever. I know that I should feel appreciative and

amazed—and Montana is beautiful, for sure—but I'm restless and bored.

I suppose this would be a great spot for me to describe what I see, the big sky and grasslands giving way to low-sweeping hills and mountains in the distance, but, um, yawn. Instead of what I see, how about what I feel? The answer to that, I'm sorry to say, is not much. Sorry, Montana!

I don't feel a thing, as if a dentist had given me too much novocaine. Numb to it all.

I only miss baseball, and my friends. What else is there?

"Meri, I mean, Will? Could you please put down the phone for a minute?"

I am in the middle of a tricky part. I have spent the last twenty minutes trying to reach the next level. I've almost got it.

My father speaks more words. There's an edge to his voice.

"One sec," I mumble.

I can sense the heat rising from his body like steam from a street grate in January. "Will!" he nearly shouts.

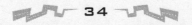

I give up the game and look up at him. "What?"

"For the past two hours, all you do is stare at that stupid phone. You don't talk, you don't even look out the window."

I slowly pivot my head and make a big point of looking out the window. Count to sixty. One full minute. "Happy now?" I ask.

He reaches for my earbuds, tries to yank them out of my head.

"Hey, ow!" I saw, jerking my head away. "What are you doing?"

"It's rude," he says. "It's like you're not even here."

But, Dad, I am here. You made sure of that. This is what you wanted, not me.

I turn up my music. Way up. I want to drown in sound.

I want him to stop talking.

Just drive.

"Give me that phone," he demands.

"No. It's my phone."

"No?" he repeats. I can see that he's surprised. I don't think I've ever said no to him before. He isn't

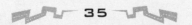

sure what to do; I can see him thinking it over. "You don't make the rules, Will. You didn't pay for that phone."

"No, Mom did," I retort.

That shuts him up for a minute. At the mention of my mother, I feel an electrical current zip through me, my nerve endings supercharged. I am wide-awake.

He feels it, too.

"I'm your father, Will," he says. "Like it or not. Now give me the phone."

He holds out his hand, gesturing for the phone.

Now, this next part is funny.

Hilarious, almost.

And it's also incredibly, fabulously stupid, because I can be such an idiot sometimes. My father has pushed me into a corner. We are in the middle of nowhere. Wi-Fi is spotty at best. Back home, at Puckett Field, there's an All-Star practice tonight—a practice that I'm missing, for a team I can't play on, because my ex-dad wants to haul me across the universe.

My right index finger presses the button on the armrest. The window slides noiselessly down and I immediately feel it, the wind and whoosh of summer heat.

I turn and can't resist, so with a flick of my wrist I pitch my phone out the window.

I look at him defiantly.

He hits the brakes, pulls over hard, stares back at me. "Will, what the hell?"

I cross my arms, thrilled. "I didn't want to be here," I tell him. "You never asked what I wanted. You didn't care."

He doesn't seem to hear me. His hands on the steering wheel tighten and release, tighten and release. It's as if he were counting to himself, trying not to react.

I say to him, "I want to be anywhere but here with you."

I fear for an instant that he might hit me. A sudden, backward smack across the face. But that's impossible. He never has, and he never will. For all my father's failings, he is not a violent man. But in his eyes I see it, a darkness crossing. I also know that I might deserve it.

He sags for a moment, as if all the air had leaked out of his body. And then the dark clouds lift, blown away by a breeze. He faces the front window, puts the car into drive, flicks on the blinker, calmly adjusts his rear mirror, and hits the gas. A mile down the road, he shakes his head and a smile, of sorts, snakes across his face.

As if he'd thought of something funny.

Great.

Another joke.

Super.

I just threw my phone out the car window somewhere in south-central Montana. The joke is on me.

About fifteen minutes later, he pulls to the side of the road, eyes fixed on the hillside. He leans over to rummage in the backseat, lifts out a pair of binoculars from under his seat. "Have you ever seen a grizzly?"

This gets my attention. The fight between us has evaporated, rolled out like a morning fog. All I want right now is to see this bear. "I thought you said they weren't in this part of Montana anymore," I say. "You said they were more west, and north, up in Glacier."

"I did say that," my father says, handing me the binoculars. "But it looks like somebody forgot to tell this guy."

"Where?" I ask.

He points at an outcropping of rocks up on the hillside, at eleven o'clock.

"I don't see it," I say.

"Keep looking," he tells me. "There."

He guides my hands, bends close to me.

I take the binoculars from my eyes, blink away the afternoon glaze, look again up the hillside. My eyes register movement. I bring the glasses again to my face, sharpen my senses, and there it is.

"I see it!" I exclaim. "A grizzly!"

"Amazing, isn't it?"

"It's so far away. How big do they get?"

"Oh, grizzlies have been known to get up to seven hundred pounds or more."

"I wish we could see one up close," I say. "That would be amazing."

My father laughs. "That's what the men on the expedition thought. But a few encounters with real grizzlies changed their minds."

He reaches into the backseat to pull out a container of water. "Thirsty?" he offers.

I drink deep, thirstier than I realized. I'm curious now, because I've always liked survival-type stories. Killer tsunamis, killer earthquakes, killer sharks, killer anything. Maybe those survival stories happened for real, but they don't feel like the dull history lessons of my father. Surprisingly, neither does this. "So what happened?" I ask. "Did anybody get killed?"

"Yeah, some bears died," my father says, "but they didn't die easily, that's for sure. In some encounters, they took shots to the shoulder, the heart, the lungs, and still kept coming."

"Wow," I say, and try to imagine what it might feel like to have a massive bear charging at me, murder in its eyes.

"You have to understand, Will, these men on the expedition were all outdoorsmen. Soldiers, hunters, tough dudes," my father says. "They took pride in their hunting skills. They were good shots. The problem was, it took them about a minute to reload their rifles. It was a complicated process, loading the powder, tamping it down, and so on. This was before the days of the repeating rifle when hunters could squeeze off a round one after the other."

We leaned against the side of the car, the sun warming my skin. All the while, I watched the burly bear move off in the distance.

"Early on the journey," my father continues, "the Indians warned them about these enormous 'white' bears. None of the men had ever seen a grizzly before. Lewis and Clark's men were eager to see a grizzly and kill it. They figured it wouldn't be so tough."

"Wrong!" I say, laughing.

Hear me, my chiefs.

I am tired.

My heart is sick and sad.

From where the sun now stands,

I will fight no more

forever.

—CHIEF JOSEPH OF THE NEZ PERCE,

SURRENDERING ON OCTOBER 5, 1877,

AFTER THE BATTLE OF BEAR PAW,

MONTANA

CHAPTER TWO

THE RIVER OF TIME

I pick up more postcards in town. My father buys a book in the gift shop and hands it to me. *Thunder Rolling in the Mountains* by Scott O'Dell and Elizabeth Hall.

Sure, whatever.

All my life he's handing me books out of nowhere.

"More Lewis and Clark?" I ask.

"Not exactly," he says. "It's the story of the Nez Perce and Chief Joseph. He was a great leader of his people." My father pauses. "There's war in the book, too. Battles and bloodshed and great sadness. Give it a chance."

"Well, as long as there's blood," I say, accepting the gift.

"The expedition members, who called themselves the Corps of Discovery, spent a lot of time with the Nez Perce, both on the way out and on the return," my father explained. "Seventy-two years later, after lies and broken treaties, the Nez Perce were kicked off their land, pursued for a thousand miles, and butchered by the United States Army." He jabs at the book with a finger. "That's when Chief Joseph gave his famous 'I will fight no more forever' speech."

"His what?" I ask, not listening.

"It's in there. Read it for yourself."

We are in the town of Fort Benton, and we're staying in a small campground for the night before heading downriver for four days through the White Cliffs of the upper Missouri. My dad keeps calling them "magical," but I don't know anything about that.

Today's a busy day, and there's a lot to do. We rent gear at a canoe outfitters, and my father makes arrangements for somebody to pick us up at Judith

Landing, eighty-eight miles away. I'm pretty excited, and my dad says I'm going to love it. We will be heading into wild, remote territory with a strict pack-it-in, pack-it-out rule—and, yes, that includes toilet paper. We actually spend time debating between a "mandatory portable toilet" or a "degradable bag system." My solution: I'm not going to poop for the next four days. It's that simple. Willpower!

Getting properly geared up is serious business, and here is where I see my father at his best. He's relaxed, calm, smart, and organized. He already packed most of the stuff we'd need in the car, but there are a lot of details to consider before heading downriver, traveling with the current, in a direction opposite from the one traveled by Lewis and Clark. We'll need sunglasses, mosquito repellent, rain gear, sunscreen, a first-aid kit—there are rattlesnakes out here—watertight containers, tent, water sandals, hiking boots, and enough food to last.

"It's not like there's a McDonald's out here," Dad says, "or any other store, until we get to Judith Landing. Think about it, Will. All this preparation is for four days, an easy eighty-eight miles floating with the current. Lewis had to plan for a trip that was eight thousand miles and took almost two and a half years."

That's a lot of toilet paper.

That night, by the fire, I crack open the book and read. My father notices, I can tell, but he says nothing. Just throws more wood on the fire, to better my light.

I am glad to be on the river, pulling a paddle through the water. This beats being trapped in the car, that's for sure. The morning air is cool and crisp. Our large canoe is filled to overflowing with gear. I can't easily describe the feeling I have on the river. Mostly it's just . . . shhh . . . a silence. A quiet that ripples inside and out, like being in a crowded elevator, a place where it doesn't feel okay to talk in a normal voice. I am excited to see the White Cliffs, but our trusty guidebook tells us that the White Cliffs section doesn't begin until Coal Banks Landing, forty-one miles downriver.

Tomorrow, Dad says. Actually he says, "We're floating into the past," and it feels true. The expedition came from the opposite direction, so we're following their path in reverse. We move through a wide, fertile valley. My father knows the names of things and points them out—cottonwood, box elder, wild rose, snowberry, sagebrush, and ash. To me, trees mostly look the same. But I like the sounds of the names in his mouth, the way the words, whispered softly, float across the water.

In this section of the river, motorboats are allowed to cruise slowly past. Fishermen, mostly, and not many. I can tell that it irks my father. "Lewis and Clark didn't have to deal with those gas-guzzlers back in the way back," he says. "Motorboats aren't allowed farther down. I'll be glad to put them behind us."

At a bend in the river, we pull over for a snack and water. My muscles already ache, but in a good way. "How you doing?" he asks me. I nod, yeah, I'm doing good.

He says, with a wave of his arm, "They camped right here in 1805. June eleventh, to be exact."

"Nice spot," I say, and it is.

He grins at me, giddy and toothy, like a boy again. "It gets better. Just wait," he promises. "Today we'll push hard, and we'll slow down as we put Fort Benton farther behind us." My father is getting younger before my eyes. We really are traveling through time. In a few minutes we are back on the water again, beating along with the current, deeper into the past. A time before everything changed. This is the world as they saw it back in 1805, for the very first time, discovering a land called America, and changing it forever.

At Decision Point, we get out for a half-mile hike. My father is eager to show me something, and I'm glad to stretch my legs.

"You okay?" he asks.

"A little sore," I say. "You?"

He gives that smile again, eyes beaming like flashlights. "I believe I could do this forever." And then he lurches forward, his long, jerky strides eating up the trail in that falling-forward way of his, until we come to a plaque titled DECISION POINT.

Uh-oh. I can sense another history lesson coming on. I want to protest, but at the same time, I can see that he's excited about this. My father wants to talk to me. It's not about baseball, it's not how the Twins are doing, or if the rookie guard on the Timberwolves is the real deal. He wants to share this, and so I try to care. After all, nobody's perfect. Unfortunately, there's not much to see, just a high point that over-looks the spot where two rivers come together. "Okay, you see that, Will?" my father asks.

Obviously, I do.

"That place, where the river divides, stopped Lewis and Clark cold. They were stumped and befuddled."

I am confused for a minute—the river divides?—then I remember that the Corps of Discovery came from the other direction. From east to west.

My father prods. "They had a decision to make: Which way?"

"They didn't know?" I ask.

"No idea," my father says, laughing. "It's not like anybody put up road signs back in those days.

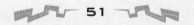

Actually, Lewis was upset because the Hidatsas never warned them about this. One river was the Missouri, leading them to the Rockies. The other one . . . who knows? It could be a dead end. President Jefferson had been clear in his instructions. He said, '*The object of your mission is to explore the Missouri River.*'"

He stands in his baggy shorts, with thick socks pulled high, and hiking boots. Like the scarecrow in *The Wizard of Oz*, he points left, and he points right, and then, grinning, he points both ways at the same time. I can see that he is happy in this place, pleased to watch me try to figure it out, urging me to think.

I frown and raise my hand, like a student in a classroom. "Hey, teacher? Is this going to be on the test?"

"I'm serious," he says.

"That's what scares me." I give up. "I don't know. Which way?"

He holds out his hands, palms to the sky. Who knows?

"Just tell me," I demand.

"No way is better, each is different," he says cryptically. "Or maybe not."

I am growing annoyed. One minute he is the scarecrow from *The Wizard of Oz*, the next he's Mr. Miyagi from *The Karate Kid*, speaking in riddles.

Sometimes I hate when he tries to teach me things. Other times, it's not so bad. Today, it's a little worse than most times.

"There's no way I can know," I finally say, "so stop asking." A new tactic to bring the lesson to a conclusion enters my skull. "Okay, how did they decide?"

"They split up, actually, and scouted in both directions," my father answers. "But they sat there stymied for a full day, making close observations of the water. The north fork was muddy, like the Missouri; the south was clear. Lewis wrote in his journal, '*Thus have our cogitating faculties been busily employed all day.*'"

"Cogitating—what?"

My father laughs. "Stop asking questions, Will, and make a choice. The point is, they didn't know,

either. No idea. One way might have been a dead end, leading nowhere. Or to dangerous encounters, starvation, disease, sure death. The other course might lead to the great passageway to the Pacific. They didn't know, *they couldn't know*—because they were the first white men to have ever stood in that exact spot. Exactly there." He points down below us. "Isn't that amazing? Doesn't it blow your mind? Think about it, Will. To stand in this exact place and not know."

I do think about it. I imagine myself in that same position, and my father is right. It *is* amazing and frightening, too. "It's like . . . the future," I suggest.

"What do you mean?"

"It's life," I say. "Every day we're more or less in this same situation, making choices."

My father picks up a rock, hurls it, hopelessly, toward the water. Or he tries to. Poor guy can't hit the side of a barn. " 'Two roads diverged in a yellow wood,' " he says.

"What?"

"It's a poem by Robert Frost," he explains. "Didn't you learn that in school yet?"

"We don't learn anything in school," I remind him. "We just take tests. Let's go back to the boat."

After dinner, at a campsite a few more miles downriver, I read for a few minutes and write a postcard that can't be mailed. On the front there's a photo of a bronze statue of Lewis, Clark, and Sacagawea that we saw in town. The men stand there looking brave and heroic, while Sacagawea sits sprawled at their feet, a baby on her back. Something about the sculpture feels false. I'm not sure why. It seems weird that the artist decided to have Sacagawea sitting on the ground, while the two white explorers stand towering above her, all brave and amazing. I mean, sure, they were mostly brave and amazing. But she was cool, too. Imagine lugging a baby halfway across the country—on your back, without diapers or a binky!

But as exhausted as I am, I don't fall sleep right away. I lie awake on top of my sleeping bag, muscles vibrating. At full dark, the birds go quiet. The silence feels almost solid, like a weight that presses down on us. If I concentrate, I can hear the water moving past, and the scratching of small animals in the under-brush. My father is crashed out beside me—he sleeps hard. He starts snoring again. I am tempted to shove a sock in his mouth. But I don't. The old man needs his sleep.

I read by flashlight until my eyelids flutter closed, the book falls to my chest, and I'm gone to dreamland.

I'm so tired right now I can barely keep my eyes open. We paddled a long way today. I don't know if I've ever heard so much silence in my life. It almost feels wrong to speak. As if, I don't know, we are trespassers or something—Big Yawn!—visiting a world where we really don't belong. Good night!

The river meanders, in no real hurry. I am dis-appointed by the absence of white water. This part of the upper Missouri is listed as a Class I rapids. That means it's an easy river to float, with riffles and small eddies, minor rapids and some obstructions—big

rocks, mostly—that are not difficult to navigate. Even so, my father insists that I wear a life vest at all times. We see other floaters from time to time, not many. We wave, we nod, but rarely speak. No one wants to shatter the dream with sharp voices, empty words. I've seen cattle grazing along the shore, and also white-tailed deer, white pelicans, bighorn sheep, and beaver. During those times, we lift our paddles and float gently downriver. I sit in the front and turn to look at my father; we lock eyes and smile. *Will you look at that, will you look at that?*

I glimpse my first sight of strange rock formations. These are called the Breaks, rocks that have been folded, faulted, uplifted, and left here, like old, dead soldiers from another, long-ago war. White sandstone cliffs begin to rise higher and higher on both sides.

It feels like we're traveling through a great stone maze built by ancient gods.

"Are there bears?" I ask during a rest stop on shore.

"Used to be lots of them," my father says. "Now, only rarely."

"Rarely?" I ask.

"Hardly ever," he says, and continues, because these are the things he knows and shares. "Bears are territorial. When it's time for the young males to leave their mamas, they have to find their own space. If there's a big old bear already there, they might fight and force the younger male out. Sometimes those young males travel great distances and get turned around, lost."

"A bear lost in the wild," I say, wondering.

"It's been known to happen, but not likely," my father says. "I wouldn't worry about it."

Too late, I think.

I'm already worried about it.

We pause on shore to stretch our legs, eat sandwiches, chomp on apples and nuts. Dad says I've been thinking about bears too much. I reply, "They call it bear country, don't they? I read it at the Interpretive Center outside of Fort Benton. What else do you want me to think about? Hedgehogs?"

He nods distractedly and focuses his attention

back to his work. My father sketches a drawing of a plant in his plain white notebook. He says it relaxes him, but I know he's trying to copy Captain Lewis, who was a student of botany. Lewis had an eye for new plants and recorded the descriptions in his famous journals. He usually sketched a quick picture, too. Dude had big talent, I'll say that.

I picked up a pamphlet about bears when we signed in at the ranger station, and I've memorized the strategies for surviving a bear encounter . . . just in case. I read it a few times each day.

SAFETY PRECAUTIONS

While you are in bear country, be aware that you might encounter a bear at any time.

1) If you encounter a grizzly, do not run. Bears are much faster than you.

2) Avoid direct eye contact—bears see that as a threat.

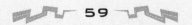

3) Walk away slowly, if the bear is not approaching.

4) If the bear charges, stand your ground—it may be bluffing and you cannot outrun it.

5) If you have bear spray, prepare to use it.

[NOTE: Bear spray is pepper spray. We do *not* have pepper spray, and it's kind of freaking me out right now.]

6) If the grizzly charges to within 25 feet, use the spray.

7) If the animal makes contact, curl up into a ball on your side, or lie flat on your stomach.

8) Try not to panic. Remain as quiet as possible until the attack ends.

9) Be sure the bear has left the area before getting up to seek help.

I feel safer in the boat, until Dad tells me that bears can swim. "What? Come on, seriously?" I reply.

He just laughs and laughs.

He won't think it's funny when the bear eats me. Who's gonna call Mom with that news?

I try to imagine it, face-to-face with a bear, and I have no idea what I'd do. I wonder if I'd be brave in that situation. I'd like to think that I'd be courageous, but I don't know.

I just don't know.

On the second night on the river, a large, dark man joins our campsite as we prepare for dinner. We are seated around the metal fire ring, feeding the fire with scrap wood we picked up during the day while foraging the waterline. The man is broad shouldered and tall, with high cheekbones and dark eyes. His tanned skin is rugged and deeply lined, and his black hair falls forward in two long, thick braids.

He wears a beaded necklace and a round, wide-brimmed hat.

My father does not say a word. The visitor looks to my father, then to me. Nods are exchanged. He rubs his large hands together, flexes his fingers as if fighting off arthritis.

"Well, are you going to introduce us?" he asks.

"Ollie," my father says, "I'd like you to meet my son, Will."

The man nods at me, his expression gentle, pleased. "Your first time on the trail?" he asks.

I look to my father, confused. *They know each other? How?*

"Um, yes . . . sir," I stammer.

My father grins, obviously enjoying my confusion. "Ollie and I go back some years. We were in grad school together. We've stayed in touch. And every few years we even manage to bump into each other along the trail."

"Did you know we'd be here?" I ask.

Ollie grins. "A little bird told me. Your father tweeted it out."

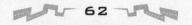

I'm surprised. *My father's on Twitter? And this guy Ollie . . . tweets?*

"We saved you some dinner," my father says. "Are you hungry?"

"Does a bear . . ." The big man pauses, winks at me, catches his words before they escape his mouth. He reconsiders and says, "Yes, please, Bruce."

I watch this exchange in amazement. I am used to seeing my father in cars and city streets, in stuffed chairs with fat books on his lap, wearing cardigan sweaters and thick-framed reading glasses. Now he is hanging out with a person who appears to be Native American. Is this my actual father? Could my father be both people at once, the bookworm and the outdoorsman, two sides of the same coin?

My father waits on our guest. Brings him a steaming plate of spaghetti, offers him water. "I expected you earlier," my father says, seated once more.

"I took a walk to visit some petroglyphs, found some old tipi rings and cairns," he says with a shrug. "Lost time, traveling in time. It was good."

Petroglyphs, I've learned on this trip, are old

drawings on rocks done by Native people. My father promises that we'll get to see some, later on down the river, maybe tomorrow.

"That hit the spot, thank you muchly," Ollie says, setting aside the empty plate. He stands, stretches, glances toward all the gear still in his boat. There's work to do.

"I'll help you," I offer, reading his mind. "My dad can do the dishes."

"Hey!" my father protests, kidding.

Ollie nods in approval. He holds up a finger, pulls a phone from the pocket of his fringed jacket, checks the sky and the surroundings, removes his hat, arranges his long braids, and takes a selfie. He punches a few keys and slides the phone back into his pocket. He notices my watchful eye and shrugs. "I wanted to get something out on Instagram before we lost the light."

A large, rough hand grips my arm. The skin is dark and weathered, like old leather. The muscles are firm and powerful.

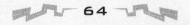

"How is everything?" Ollie asks me in an urgent whisper. He glances in the direction of my father, who cannot hear us. "Any news?"

For the past twenty minutes, I've helped Ollie set up camp. We hauled gear from his boat, pitched a tent, all as the evening sky glowed bright before the dying of the light, mosquito time, dusk, and then full dark.

Now his big paw is squeezing my arm. He looks at me with dark, probing eyes. "Your father seems distracted," Ollie says. "I've been worried ever since—"

I shake my head. I don't know what he's asking me. "What?" I manage to say.

Once again I watch him swallow his words. His head tilts to the side, and he pulls back slightly, loosening the grip on my arm. He turns from me to point high up the White Cliffs. "Eagles nest up there sometimes. Maybe tomorrow along the river you'll spot one." He winks at me. "It's good for the soul."

I stare at him with wonder, still trying to process what's going on between us. A moment ago, he

seemed so intense. So concerned. Telling me that he was worried. But the next minute he's talking about eagles, as if he were no longer interested in my answer.

He saw something in my reaction. He thinks I know something. But I'm in the dark.

We sit around the fire ring. Two men and I. There are other campers here along the river, but folks keep to themselves, move silently, talk in hushed voices. Ollie pokes the fire with a stick and speaks . . .

"My people, the Nez Perce, crossed this river not far from here in 1877. They hoped the Crow would join them in their fight against the U.S. Army, but the Crow turned their backs." He snaps the stick in half, feeds the fire. Ollie's voice is flat like the prairie. He doesn't look at us. It's like he's talking to the fire, but I know that his words are meant for my ears.

Ollie looks up at me. The firelight shines on his face. "The past haunts this place. There are ghosts around every corner, under every rock." He names the tribes that have occupied the Upper Missouri in the past: Blackfeet, Crow, Cree. "Other tribes would come to hunt buffalo, the Lakota, Arikara, Hidatsa, Shoshone, and my people, the Nez Perce."

"But times change," my father comments. Our mood has changed, too. A cool breeze blows. The men seem wistful, thinking about what has been lost.

"For my people," Ollie tells me, "it was as if the earth were shrinking. The whites came and they came and they kept coming. As numerous as the stars. We were like the deer grazing on the grass. The whites were like the grizzly."

"The wheel of progress rolls over everything in its path, indifferent," my father observes. I poke the fire with a stick, wishing for marshmallows. A s'more would hit the spot right about now. He likes talking like that. I'm used to it by now. When I was little, he brought me to the college where he teaches. Maybe he got stuck with me for the day, couldn't find a babysitter, or maybe he wanted me to see him at work. I remember sitting there with my coloring book and crayons, my legs kicking the air, in the back of a big lecture hall. There were so many students in that room. My dad stood up front, pacing, pointing, yammering away. I didn't understand a word of it. Nowadays when he gets going like that, I understand exactly half of it.

Progress!

Ollie rises, goes to his tent, and returns with a leather sack with a cap on the end. "Whiskey," Ollie explains. "A dram for every man."

"Let's be civilized. Fetch us two cups, Will," my father asks. I am happy to do it.

"Lewis brought one hundred and twenty gallons of whiskey on the journey," my father informs me. "They had to ration it very carefully, a little bit here and there. The men enjoyed their drink after a long day."

Ollie pours brown liquid into their cups. "Sorry, Will," he says, "you're just a pup."

"On the expedition, two soldiers tapped the reserves while on guard duty and got drunk," my father says.

"They flogged them for it," Ollie notes with a nod.

"Flogged?" I ask.

"They whipped them, Will. One hundred lashes for Private John Collins, and fifty for the other man, whose name I forget," my father replies.

"Hugh Hall," Ollie remembers.

"Ah, Hugh Hall," my father says. He lifts his cup and sips, toasting our guest's good memory. "Remember, Will, this was a military operation. They were headed into hostile territory. Discipline was important. So, yes, they whipped them. Cruel but effective."

I try to imagine the pain that comes from a whipping. The skin cracked, the flesh raw and bloodied. "You never hit me," I say.

Ollie raises a finger. "Not yet," he jokes. The two men clank metal cups, and we all laugh. After a long while, Ollie pulls out a beat-up fiddle from his pack. He asks, "Tell me, Will, do you know the difference between a violin and a fiddle?"

I have no idea.

Ollie smiles. "If you can imagine somebody spilling beer on it, then it's a fiddle."

They laugh again, cackling round the campfire,

sparks flying. I like to see my father in this new light. He seems happier and looser and, to be honest, easier to like. I wonder where this guy has been hiding all my life. Ollie plays soft and low, haunting melodies that float up to the moon. A wolf or coyote howls in the distance. My father says that one member of the Corps, a half-French, half–Omaha Indian named Pierre Cruzatte, played his fiddle on many nights during the expedition. Listening to Ollie, I understand why. The music, for a moment, seems to tame the wilderness; things do not seem so fierce and remote anymore. At the end of one tune, a camper from a faraway fire calls out, "Very nice, thank you!"

Another cries, "'Free Bird'!" and a spasm of laughter ripples through the darkness.

I look at my father. *He does not seem worried in the least.* He appears happy. So what was Ollie talking about? *How is everything?* he had asked me. Why would he ask that?

You know how people say that Disneyland is a magical place. Well, not compared to here. And at night—the stars! Save this card,

please. Save all the cards I send! Also,
getting sick of peanut butter. Not really!

The absolute worst thing about sleeping in a tent is
when you've got to get up to pee. There you are nice
and toasty, and next you've got to unzip the sleeping
bag, fumble around for a flashlight, unzip the tent,
and step out into the cool night air. It's as dark as a
closet. On this night, I don't go very far; there's no
one around. I spread my legs, yawn, scarcely awake,
and let out a steady stream.

Just as I finish—standing in my boxers and
socks—I hear something moving in the under-
growth. I turn my head but register only a formless
black mass in the brush. My eyes can't focus on any
object. It's all a midnight haze. But I hear it, the heavy
footfalls of a large animal, as if death were stalking
me from the shadows. I smell, or imagine that I smell,
the beast's wet fur and its hot, foul breath.

The bear pauses in the space between my heart-
beats. I can sense its nature as it stares at me. I do
not call for my father; I do not slowly, cautiously step
away. I only stand there, frozen with fear, heart

hammering, useless. And then it rumbles off, twigs snapping. Gone like a ghost. Vanished. The bear retreats back into the dark depths, fading into the black. Rank and cruel and wild.

Something terrible is going to happen. I can feel it in my bones. Sooner or later, I tell myself, I will have to be brave. I know that this is true. And I know as I wait here, trembling and afraid, that one day soon I will face the bear.

I sleep late and awake to full light, to see that Ollie has already packed most of his things into the tandem boat. His smaller, single craft is gone, yet here is Ollie—sitting by our makeshift kitchen, a mini butane camp stove—sipping from a coffee cup.

"The sun also rises," Ollie says, curiously, in greeting.

I look around. "Where's my dad?"

"He went ahead," Ollie answers. "He decided to let you sleep."

He decided.

That figures.

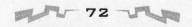

He didn't give me a vote.

He left without me. This new circumstance doesn't put me in a good mood.

I yawn, stretch, wipe gunk from my eyes, the crust from last night's uneasy sleep. I look back at the tent, half expecting to see the bear. Waiting, watching. Of course, it's not there.

Ollie stands, splashes the remains of his coffee to the ground. "Tell you what, young Will. How would you like some pancakes, Nez Perce style?"

"Sounds great," I say, suddenly aware of my hunger.

"Tell you what. Pack up the tent and put your things in order while I organize the meal," Ollie says. He pauses for moment, assessing me. "You know how?"

I lie and say that I do.

Ten minutes later, it becomes true in the doing. I teach myself how.

The pancakes are waiting when I'm done. Ollie watches as I take the first bite. "Good," I tell him truthfully. Not exactly Denny's, but in a setting like this, everything tastes better. As I eat, Ollie unbraids and brushes out his long, thick hair.

He fusses with his front forelock, stylishly sweeping it up and to the back.

"Going for a different look today?" I joke.

Ollie frowns. "It is the style of my people. Goes back generations. Don't you like it?"

"I definitely do," I say.

Ollie begins to re-braid his hair, fingers moving quickly and effortlessly. "We'll hike to the Hole in the Wall today. You'll see Eagle Rock, Dark Butte, Citadel Rock."

"What about my father?" I ask.

"We camp tonight at Slaughter River. He'll be there."

Slaughter River?

Sounds swell.

We are on the water. Ollie takes the rear, which is always the position for the stronger, more experienced paddler. I can feel his long, powerful strokes propelling the boat forward. It is my task to keep my eyes

on the water, to call out warnings when I spy rocks and other potential dangers ahead—watching for sandbars, whirlpools, floating debris.

I lift my paddle and point it to warn Ollie about a huge rock that's just under the surface. Suddenly, he veers the boat directly for it.

"No, no," I cry, waving my hand. "Over, over!"

Ollie quickly rudders us to the right, gives four short strokes on the left side, and we skirt the boulder by inches.

"Pup, are you trying to get me wet?" Ollie demands in a gruff voice. "What are you doing up there?"

"I was pointing out the rock," I explain.

Ollie shakes his head, frowning. "On the river, a paddler always points toward the clear path. Never to the obstacle. Understand?"

I nod. "Sorry, I didn't know."

"It's exactly like life," he says. A moment later, he splashes me with the paddle and asks, "Say, Will, how's the weather up there? Looks like rain to me." He chuckles, pleased with his joke.

It's a strange feeling, to be alone with this stranger. Yet now that my father is away, this trip feels more like an adventure. I like Ollie, though it's hard to put my finger on why. He's different, I guess. Cool and detached, like a bird that watches from the sky. My thoughts keep returning to my father. How could he have left without a word of explanation? I surprise myself when this thought scrolls across my mind: *He doesn't care.* And for that moment, I receive the message as if it were true.

He doesn't care. Not really.

For the next twenty minutes, I paddle furiously, leaning into each stroke until my back stiffens. Spent, I rest the paddle across my knees and let the current do the work. The river has gone silent, no more motorboats, and the scenery becomes increasingly fantastical, with strange rock formations appearing out of nowhere. Rock walls tower above us. Weird shapes suddenly appear. I find myself turning back to Ollie and saying dumb things like, "Gosh, wow," or, "It feels like a dream."

We pull out when Ollie says that he wants to show

me the site of an old cabin. "Pulling out" is river talk, I've learned, and the opposite of "putting in." We drag our boat ashore and walk a little ways. Ollie hands me an energy bar. The site is not much to look at, only partial walls remain. But Ollie circles it with a kind of reverence. "They say it was owned by an old wolf trapper and horse thief back in the middle 1800s," Ollie announces. "There's a lot of history here." He closes his eyes, as if to better feel it: the presence of the past pressing in all around us.

"My people crossed this river, not too far, near Cow Island," he says, flicking his wrist, "during the war of 1877. Did they teach you that in school? I'd guess not, eh?"

I shake my head.

"Do you mind if I try to teach you something?" he asks. "Or would you prefer to remain blissfully ignorant?"

And because he asks, or because it's *him*, I tell Ollie that I don't mind. He explains, "The Nez Perce were pushed off their land and chased by General Howard, the one-armed man, for five months"—he

sweeps an arm in a long, slow gesture—"across more than one thousand miles. They hoped to reach Canada, to join up with Sitting Bull, who had just defeated Custer." Ollie checks the sky; his eye follows the flight of a bird.

I ask, "Why didn't the army just let them go?"

Ollie thinks for a moment. "The Great Spirit Chief must have been looking some other way on that particular day," he decides.

I'm not sure if he's teasing me, testing me, or if he's serious. Ollie keeps me guessing.

"Anyway, they never made it. Forty miles short of freedom, and after the senseless deaths of many—on both sides—Chief Joseph was forced to surrender."

"'I will fight no more forever,'" I say, repeating the words from the chief's famous speech. I've been reading up, and I am pleased to show off my knowledge. It connects us.

Ollie nods in approval. "No more forever," he repeats in a dry whisper.

"Is that why you come here?" I ask.

"Beats me." Ollie grins and shakes his head. "My birth name is Ollokot. My parents named me after the brother of Chief Joseph, war leader of the Wallowa band of Nez Perce. Ollokot was killed in the Battle of Bear Paw—and I believe it broke Joseph's heart."

He continues, "I am also a Lewis and Clark enthusiast, like your father. That's what first brought us together. I love the history of it, the days gone by, what one scholar, Greil Marcus, calls 'the old, weird America.'"

"Weird America?" I ask.

"You saw the last election. Don't you agree?" Ollie says, laughing. "The more you learn, the weirder this country gets."

We return to our boat and paddle on, borne by the current. "I think I heard a bear last night," I confess over my shoulder.

Ollie does not comment. I wonder, even, if he hears me. After a pause, I tell him how I rose to go the bathroom and heard something large and dangerous moving around in the darkness.

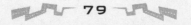

"Did you discover tracks?" he asks.

Tracks? I hadn't thought to look.

I shake my head.

We are silent for so long that I assume the conversation has been dropped. But Ollie finally muses, "It is unlikely that a bear would come into our camp in that place. There used to be many here, but no more. But don't ask me, I'm just an investment banker from Brooklyn."

"Really?" I ask.

"And truly," he replies. "I wear a suit and tie and everything. You should see me in a double-breasted blue blazer. It's hideous."

His laughter bounces off the canyon walls.

I'm a little disappointed. I was hoping for more— I don't know—wisdom. It was probably unfair of me to expect it.

Maybe Ollie senses my feelings, because he says, "I live in the city, Will. But my roots are here. My grandfather, well, he was a great one. He knew all the old ways. He would have said that you were visited by a spirit animal."

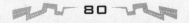

I lift my paddle out of the water and turn to look at him.

Ollie explains, "Our people believe in spirits, called *weyekins*, that come in the form of visions. Usually it occurs when one is on a quest." He pauses, considering. "Are you on a quest, young William?"

I shrug. "I don't think so."

Ollie tilts his head as if he doesn't believe me. "You are on a journey," he says. "A quest is part of every journey."

"I'm on *vacation*," I tell him. "I wouldn't call it a journey."

"And yet the bear spirit came to you in the night," Ollie says. "Unless you think it was mistaken? Perhaps it visited the wrong tent?"

"I guess it was just my imagination," I say, not entirely sure. I return to paddling, my back to him.

"The old ones believe that an animal spirit can come in a dream, or as a vision," Ollie explains. "It comes to bestow the animal's power. It is a great thing, William. A gift you must accept."

"A gift?" I say. "I don't think getting eaten by a bear is a gift!"

"You have a point." Ollie smiles.

"So what do you believe?" I ask.

"Will," he answers, "I live in a three-story brownstone in Brooklyn Heights, New York. I take a train to work in the morning, and I make far too much money on Wall Street. I'm divorced, and my kids are gone. My big pleasure is going to see the Knicks play basketball at Madison Square Garden. I have season tickets, good seats, and that team breaks my heart every year." For a moment there is only silence. We drift on the river. And I wait. "You asked before why I come here, that's probably the reason. I'm not sure what I believe in anymore. But out here, things seem more"—he pauses—"possible."

"So you do think that the bear—"

Ollie rests the paddle across his lap. He leans in. "If the bear wanted to eat you, Will, you'd have been eaten. It would not be a difficult matter. Listen. According to the old ways of my people, the bear came to offer you its power. Its strength and courage," he says, speaking slowly, "for your long journey."

"Okay, then," I say. "What's my quest?"

Ollie laughs out loud, a kind of hoot. He says, "That's why you go on the journey—to find out!"

Later that afternoon, Ollie points a finger to a great bird circling above. "There's your eagle," he says. "Let's drift awhile."

We don't paddle, we don't talk.

The great bird sweeps across the river, riding the winds from cliff to cliff, out in front of us by a hundred feet.

"She's hunting," Ollie whispers.

And now down she comes, fast and low, closer and closer to our boat. I can clearly see her white head, the way the wind ruffles her wing feathers. Her talons come forward and, *smack*, *splash*, she hits the water and then rises up, rises up. The eagle holds a large fish by the head and carries it away.

And I was there to see it.

To feel it.

My father is already at the Slaughter River campsite, pants rolled up to his shins, pale feet soaking in the river. He is all smiles and comes to help us unload the boat. Shakes Ollie's hand. I find the whole act irritating.

"You left me," I say.

Ollie glances at my father, lifts a pack, and gives us privacy by walking away.

"You were sleeping," my father answers. "I thought you needed the rest."

"Whatever," I grumble.

"Don't be mad." He reaches for my arm. I pull away. "To be honest, I wanted time alone to do some writing," he explains. "I woke up early and . . ."

He looks down, rubs the back of his neck, digs a little hole in the sand with the heel of his foot. "I'm sorry, Will. Okay? Tomorrow we'll be back in the boat together. I just thought that—"

"No, I'm good," I interrupt. "I like floating with Ollie. It's better. We go faster. He tells me stories. He talks to me. He listens."

Zing. I can see that my arrow hits its mark.

"Sure," my father says, "of course. That's fine."

"I want to call Mom," I say.

"First things first," he says. "Let's get camp set up."

"Why not now?" I argue.

"Because I said no," my father snaps. There's an edge to his voice. A threat, almost. I push past him, not even bothering to help with the gear.

He can be such a creep sometimes.

That night, we camp where the Corps of Discovery camped more than two hundred years ago. Meriwether Lewis and his men. Under the same starry skies, staring into the same fire, beside the same chalky cliffs.

I want to tell my father about the bald eagle Ollie and I saw. And the pronghorn. And about the hard, dangerous hike to the top of the Hole in the Wall trail. How it looked so tiny from the river, but was twice my size when we finally got up to it after some dicey scrambling. How Ollie had pointed out ponderosa pines and cottonwoods. Instead, I ate and yawned and climbed into my sleeping bag. Dog tired. My heart confused.

My spirit animal did not visit during the night.

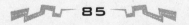

The next afternoon, we pull out at Judith Landing. Ollie says good-bye. He is heading farther east down the Breaks toward James Kipp Park. I am sad to see him go, this banker from New York with Nez Perce blood flowing through his veins, who takes selfies and scrolls through Twitter and Instagram. He isn't exactly how I expected him to be, but then again, I never expected him at all.

"Young Will," he says to me. "Come to New York and I'll take you to an NBA game. How would you like that?"

I look to my father, who raises his eyebrows as if to say, *Hey, maybe someday.*

"I've never been to New York," I say.

"Well, maybe your father can fix that," Ollie says. He places his big paw on my shoulder. "You are a good river man and a sturdy paddler. I see that you keep your own journal. That's good. Make a record of what you see and feel. It will help you remember things—especially your new friend, Ollie!"

He pulls me into a hug. "Be fierce like the bear,

your spirit animal," he tells me with a wink. "And don't ever forget that Captain Lewis could have never reached the Pacific Ocean without the kindness and generosity of the Native people. When we celebrate Lewis and Clark, we also honor the Native tribes who allowed them to pass."

Finally, Ollie gives my father a lingering hug. Then he pulls back, arms out, hands clasped on my father's shoulders. "You've got this," he says. "Be strong, be brave, and keep in touch, my friend. Write well, and finish that book!"

My father doesn't want me to notice, so he turns away to wipe something from his eye.

But I see everything.

Be strong, be brave, and keep in touch.

I wonder if my father might be going away.

The last I see of Ollie, he is holding an imaginary basketball. He bends low, pretending to dribble, then pivots to shoot a turnaround jumper. He points a finger at me, grinning. "Swish," he says, laughing. "Every time."

If we do not find
[the Shoshones], I fear
the successful issue of our voyage
will be very doubtful.

—MERIWETHER LEWIS

CHAPTER THREE

AN ILLEGAL GIRL

After pulling out at Judith Landing, four days after first putting in, my father and I catch a pre-arranged shuttle bus back to Fort Benton, where we'd left the car. As a treat, he decides to spring for the swanky Grand Union Hotel in the heart of downtown. It's a beautiful old brick building near the river. I am grateful to have a television and a big, soft bed with sheets and pillows. A working toilet isn't half bad, either. I take a long, hot bath in one of those old-fashioned tubs with feet, and I wash my hair twice. When I'm done, I find a note on the dresser. "Will, I nipped out for a quick ramble around town. Don't disappear. Dinner at 6:00. Love, Dad."

I sit on the bed, half dressed, find the remote, and surf the channels. There's nothing on. Or, I should say, nothing interests me. Not after the river. I'm not ready to return to the zombie life just yet, though I do miss my phone. I go to the window, glance up and down upon the street. And there she is, crossing the street—the girl I saw in Bismarck with her dog. How could that be? It seems impossible. A minute later, I'm fully dressed. I scribble, "Back soon!" at the bottom of my father's note and head out the door, the spare room key and a twenty-dollar bill in my back pocket.

The town looks nice, but I'm not interested in shopping. Across the way there's a small park with picnic tables and a statue of a dog. That's where I find the girl, sitting cross-legged on a blanket. There's no doubt that it's the girl from Bismarck, because the same gigantic black dog lazes on the grass beside her. The dog's eyes follow me as I walk past them on my way to the statue, as if that were my true destination.

I finally pluck up enough courage. I greet the dog first, letting it smell my hand before reaching to pet it. "Your dog is ginormous!" I say, kneeling before her. The big animal gives itself to me, glad to be scratched. It slobbers, openmouthed, with a kind of laughing grin. I awkwardly try to wipe the dog's slime from my sleeve onto the grass. The girl offers a light laugh. "He is messy," she says.

Up close, I can see that she is older than I am by a few years, not too much, but enough to place us in different worlds. She is still, however, too young to be here alone. By her side, there's a ratty, dark orange backpack in addition to the cloth bag I saw her carrying back on the streets of Bismarck. A sleeping bag. Her hands reach into the enormous cloth bag and she produces an assortment of beaded jewelry, which she spreads before me on the blanket.

"Do you want to . . . purchase?" she asks uncertainly.

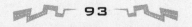

"You made these?" I ask.

"Yes, for sale," she says, in a way that tells me that English is not her first language.

She holds up a leather bracelet, displays it across her own slender wrist. It is simply made, with two green beads. I think of my mother. "How much?" I ask.

She looks at me with round, wide-set eyes. I see, I think, some sadness there. She isn't sure of how to answer. I pull out my money, the twenty-dollar bill. "Is this enough?"

She reaches for it hungrily. "Oh, *sí, sí,* yes," she says. Now her face beams, and I see in that flash of happiness her full beauty. Even so, there is faint discoloring around her left eye from an old bruise and scratch marks on her wrists. I think she is wearing the same clothes that I saw on her before. The girl drops the bracelet into my hands.

"I was wondering, do you have a phone?" I ask. "That I could borrow? Just to make a quick call?"

She shakes her head.

How can a person not have a phone? Are we the only two people on the planet without one?

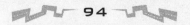

"I saw you before, about five days ago," I begin, and I describe the day I saw her in Bismarck. Her eyes widen, surprised and delighted.

"Oh yes, I . . . I . . ." She holds up her thumb.

"Hitchhike?"

"Yes, I hitch!" She shrugs, looks around, as if for the first time. "Now we are here."

"Isn't it dangerous?" I ask.

"Not with Paco," she says, scratching the black dog's ears. "My protector."

"Where are you going?"

She begins to answer, but shakes her head as if thinking better of it. "I have a cousin Alejandro," she confesses. "I am . . . *seeking* for him."

A quest, I think.

"I'm Will," I tell her.

"Maria Rosa," she replies, and holds out her hand to me. She is not afraid anymore. Not of me, at least.

"It's nice to meet you," I say, like the spazzy gentleman that I am. "Will you be here later?"

She isn't sure. Gives a shrug.

I think of what might cause her to stay. "I just

thought that—I can get more money," I say. "You could sell me a necklace, maybe?"

Then I ask, "Are you hungry?"

She strokes the dog along the length of its spine. "Him," she says. "Only Paco."

This is a statue of Shep, an important dog in the town of Fort Benton. They say that Shep hung out at the train station every day for five years waiting for his master to return. Unfortunately, his master was dead, but Shep made it into *Ripley's Believe It or Not!* Worst of all, Shep died when he got hit by a train. True fact! Old, weird America!

"Don't disappear like that," my father scolds when I enter the room. "I was worried."

"Then we're even," I counter.

"I left you a note," he explains. "I needed to find the library, make some calls."

"Who'd you call?"

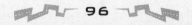

"Susan," he answers stiffly.

The girlfriend.

It is not a topic we discuss much.

"Well, I want to call Mom," I tell him.

"She's out," he says.

"What?"

"I tried her before and left a message."

Before I can process this, he asks, "Where were you anyway? I said dinner at six."

"Out looking around," I say. "There's a statue of a dog in the park."

"Shep," my father answers. "The famous sheepdog. You can tell me about it over dinner."

We eat like kings in the hotel restaurant. He talks about our "agenda," a hike along the Lolo Trail, maybe even some white water if we have time; I am barely listening. My thoughts are on Maria Rosa. It will be dusk soon. *Why can't I find the nerve to tell him?*

I pull the bracelet from my pocket.

"I bought this for Mom. Do you think she'll like it?"

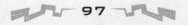

"You did? Why, that's not necess—" he begins to say, then catches himself. "That's nice. I'm sure your mother will love it."

He cuts into his steak.

I munch my chicken Parm. It's not as good as Angela's, the sauce tastes funny, but I'm starving.

A difficult silence passes. It seems to happen whenever I mention my mother. I hate it because I never know what to say. It's as if he wants me to pretend that I don't have a mother.

"I saw that girl again," I say.

"What girl?"

I tell him about Maria Rosa and the big dog. As my story deepens, my father grows interested, asks questions. I can see his concern. "She hitchhiked all the way from Bismarck?" he asks. "That's not safe. How old is this girl?"

"Older than me," I say. "She's Mexican, I think. Or, I don't know, I'm not sure." And then I say, "I think maybe she's homeless or something. Like a runaway."

In that moment, my father signals to the waiter for the check. He signs it, and we are up and

moving. "Show me," he says, striding across the carpeted lobby to the front door. "Take me to where you saw this girl."

We find her, after some searching, on a bench overlooking the river. Paco is off leash, sniffing around at the water's edge, but when we approach his head rears up and he positions himself between the potential threat and his master.

"Hello, Paco. Remember me?" I say, once again allowing the dog to smell my outstretched hand.

"*Está bien*, Paco," Maria Rosa says in a soft voice. "No worries." The faithful dog sniffs my father and then, satisfied, goes to the girl's side. She watches us with a guarded expression, arms crossed. I make introductions. Maria nods, wary. I take a seat on the bench while my father regards the river, hands on his hips. "Warm night," he says pointlessly. With a tilt of his chin, he gestures to Maria's things. "Are you camping out?"

Maria sits expressionless. She crosses her legs. Looks down and away.

My father squats on his haunches, waits for Maria Rosa to look him in the eye. He says in a soft voice, "Do you have nowhere to go?" He pauses, struggling to find the words in Spanish, "*¿Qué tienes—*"

She clips the rope to the dog's collar. A signal that the interview is over. She reaches for the strap of her backpack.

"I only want to help," my father says, lifting his hands, palms out. "*Quiero . . . ayudar,*" he says.

"Please," I say.

A flicker passes across Maria's face. It softens, ever so slightly. The wall comes down. She nods, as if to say, *I will listen, no more than that.*

It is a beginning.

For the next ten minutes, they talk back and forth, mostly in English, with Spanish words sprinkled throughout. I do not say a word. Instead, I rub my hands through Paco's thick, matted fur. Under it, I feel the dog's ribs. Paco hasn't been eating enough.

My father's voice carries kindness in it. Gentleness. He touches the area around his own right eye, asks

about the bruise on Maria's face. She does not say much, but it is enough. "How old are you?" he asks.

She flashes five fingers on her forearm three times. "*Quince*," she answers.

"Where is home?" he asks.

She shakes her head, and the hardness returns to her face. She won't go back.

I say, "She has a cousin."

My father takes a deep, long breath. Inhale, exhale. He looks back toward the yellow lights in the hotel's high windows. A soft rain begins to fall. He rises, "Well, you cannot stay here. Come, *por favor*."

He begins to lift her backpack, hand grabbing for the strap, and pauses. "Will you let me help you?" he asks.

Her thin fingers reflexively go to her belly. She looks at Paco, as if the dog holds the answer. Maybe it does. At last, yes, she whispers, *sí*, and then this: *gracias*.

We walk toward the hotel, together.

"We'll sort this out," my father says, as if speaking to himself. "But first, we'll find you a safe place

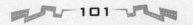

to sleep. A place," he says, leaning to scratch Paco's head, "that accepts dogs."

I first learned about Sacagawea back in elementary school. Our librarian read a picture book to us. The main idea was that she was a brave, wise Indian girl who helped Lewis and Clark on their journey. You know, a "good," friendly Indian. But on my summer trip, I learned a different story. First, Sacagawea was basically a slave, but nobody called it that. I mean, she grew up with the Shoshones, but was kidnapped by the Hidatsa tribe at around age ten. When she turned thirteen, the Hidatsas sold Sacagawea to a part-French, part-Indian fur trapper named Toussaint Charbonneau. My father, who knows all this stuff, says that in older books they commonly referred to Sacagawea as Charbonneau's "wife." Even the Corps soldiers did. But the undeniable fact is he bought her—purchased another living person. That isn't marriage—it's slavery. When Sacagawea was fifteen and pregnant, Charbonneau offered his services as a translator for the Corps of Discovery up at Fort Mandan. Neither Lewis nor Clark liked Charbonneau very much. They thought he was a jerk, actually. But they figured Sacagawea might be useful when they met up with the Shoshones, since she spoke the language. She was going to be their "free pass" through hostile territory. Can you believe that? To me, even though Sacagawea seemed like a tough girl, it's not like she ever had a choice. I feel pretty bad for her, to tell you the truth. Nobody asked what she wanted.

I wait up in our room while my father gets Maria settled. He looks tired and drawn when he returns. He tosses me a bag of peanut M&M'S. "Gotta love vending machines," he says.

"How is she?" I ask.

He sits heavily in the chair by the window. "I was able to get her a room for the night," he says. "Tomorrow will be a new day."

"What about Paco?"

"She would not part with that dog," he says, smiling at the memory. "Very clear about that. She struggles at times with English, but she can make herself understood, that's for sure. It took some persuasion, but . . . the people in the hotel . . . are kind. They made an exception."

"So what now?" I ask.

"We are going to take a little detour," he tells me. "Try to find that cousin. She has an address scribbled on an old index card. No phone number. Dillon, Montana. I know the area, it's not far from the Lemhi Pass, so it works out well, actually. If that's all right with you?"

This is definitely all right. "Yes," I say.

"It's all a little confused," my father continues, as if talking out the details helped him sort through the facts. "Maria claims they were last together a couple of years ago, but she doubts he lives in the same place anymore—a letter she wrote was returned, undeliverable. But it's a start."

"Can we ask the police for help?" I suggest.

My father tilts his head from side to side. He goes to the bathroom, returns with a plastic cup of water. "I suspect she's here illegally," he says. "The police may be the last thing she needs right now."

"Illegally?" I ask.

"We don't know her entire story, Will. I suspect that Maria Rosa may not have entered the country legally," my father explains. "If she encounters the police, she could be deported."

These are deep, complex thoughts. A little over my head. I decide to trust my father.

"If she's illegal—" I begin to say.

"She's scared, Will. Out of her mind. She's a fifteen-year-old girl, all alone."

I sit, frowning, pensive.

My father says, "Lewis and Clark went looking for America. But America isn't a place you find, Will, it's a place we continually make anew—every single day—by how we treat each other. Think of the poem on the Statue of Liberty."

Of course, I don't even know that it comes with a poem.

He closes his eyes and recites: "*'Give me your tired, your poor, / Your huddled masses yearning to be breathe free . . .'*"

I listen to my father. I don't fully understand what he's talking about, but it feels right. When I picture Maria, all I see is a girl who needs our help. It seems simple, really. "I guess this isn't the trip you expected," I offer.

My father laughs. "No, no, it isn't. You did good, Will. This is the least we can do. Life happens, right? That's what John Lennon said. When you are busy making other plans."

I yawn and stretch out on the soft, expansive bed. It sure beats sleeping on the hard ground. Before nodding off, I ask, "Who's John Lennon?"

He cries, "Ack!" and throws a pillow at me.

I love doing that to him. It makes my father crazy when I act like I never heard of the Beatles. Pretty funny, if you ask me. His buttons are so easy to push.

Paco takes up most of the backseat. His breath is hot and a thread of slobber drips from the corner of his

mouth. Even so, it's cozy to have him beside me. We are headed south, driving down Route 87, then 15, through Helena, Butte, and on toward Dillon and the Beaverhead River in search of Alejandro, Maria's cousin. She claims that she has not seen him in two years. They've lost touch. Maria does not say so, but she seems nervous, picking at the fabric of her shirt. Mostly, she stares out the front windshield and remains quiet.

I am half sleeping with Paco sprawled out against me. My father and Maria Rosa talk softly. I close my eyes and hear the wipers swish mechanically across the windshield, the whoosh of wheels on wet cement. It is raining hard. A blast of summer rain, and a nice break from the July heat. I am glad this girl is with us, dry and safe. Glad for my father, too. Glad for everything.

There's an urgency to his voice. He says, "When we find Alejandro, please stay with him, build a home, someplace safe. ¿*Comprende?* Do you understand?"

I tilt my head to see Maria's profile, broad nose and full lips. "*Sí*," she answers. "Yes, I understand."

"Family is everything," my father says. "People and places come and go, but family—blood, you know"—he searches for the right word—"*rojo*, blood," he repeats. "*Familia es todo*. Without *familia*, we are lost and alone. It is all just . . . emptiness."

"*Mi primo* is . . . difficult," she says.

"He is all you have right now," my father counters. "Let's hope that he opens his arms to you"—and he nods to her—"and the baby."

The baby?

She lightly touches her belly with her fingertips, turns away to stare into the afternoon deluge. My father is silent. The wipers swoosh and thump, back and forth, back and forth, like the beat of a sad song.

How could Maria be pregnant? She's so young. Where's the father? I can't understand her life; it's like a foreign land to me.

We are headed into new country, a land unknown to me. I see open fields, low hills, sagebrush and brown grasses, fir and pines. Off to the west in the distance, out my right window, I see steep, snow-capped mountains.

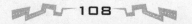

"*Familia es todo*," Maria says in a whispering echo, almost like a prayer, almost as if she were trying to convince herself.

Though I am invisible in the backseat, I nod in agreement. I think of my mother. This is the longest time we've ever been separated. I am happy here on our journey. It feels good. An adventure. But I will be glad when I am home again.

We drive on.

"Hello? Bruce?" Her voice sounds uncertain, the signal weak.

"Mom?"

"Will!" she exclaims. "I'm so glad you called. I'm sorry, I was sleeping. Hold on one sec."

Sleeping? It's lunchtime.

"Are you still in bed?"

"No, I must have just dozed off on the couch," she says.

I'm confused. "Aren't you at work?"

What day is today anyway? I've lost track of time.

"No." She sniffs. "I have a little cold. I took a sick

day. The medicine knocked me out. But tell me," she says, her voice a purr, groggy and gentle, "how are you?"

I begin to tell my mother everything, but it's impossible. "Did you get my postcards?"

"Postcards? No, when did you send them?"

Oh yeah. Just this morning, I remember, before I climbed into the backseat with a gargantuan, slobbering dog. No wonder she didn't get my postcards yet. "Today," I reply.

"Oh," she answers. "The U.S. Postal Service is fast, but it's not *that* fast."

There is a soft silence between us.

"Where are you?"

"I'm standing outside of a Dairy Queen in a town called Dillon, Montana," I explain.

"Yum, get a vanilla shake for me!" she says, then shifts to, "Are you getting along with your father?"

"Sure," I answer. "You know Dad, he's limited, but he means well." It's a description I've learned from her. "We're on a quest."

"A quest?"

"Sort of," I say. "It's a long story."

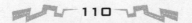

I hear her yawn.

"Will, I'm so glad you called. This is just a bad time—this cold," she corrects herself, "it's knocked me for a loop."

"That's okay, Mom," I answer. "I just wanted to say hi."

I recall the last time we spoke. I was walking out the door and she called after me, *I love you.*

I didn't even look back.

"I love you, Mom," I tell her now. "I bought you a present!"

"You did? Oh, I love presents. I can't wait to see it."

There's a voice in the background. Someone whispering to my mother.

"Is someone with you?" I ask.

"Oh, yes. Aunt Barbara is visiting."

"Aunt Barbara? From Chicago? That's strange," I say. "She never visits."

There's a pause, another yawn, and my mother adds, "We decided it would be fun, so she jumped on a plane and now she's here."

"Too bad you have a cold," I say.

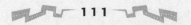

"It's nothing," she reassures me. "Just the sniffles."

I can see my father watching me through the Dairy Queen window. His expression is curious, alert. He's seated across from Maria Rosa, who is biting into an enormous burger. I hold up a finger, signaling one minute.

"I should go," I say.

"Will?" she says, her voice rising in question. "You confused me at first. This is your father's number. He texted a few days ago to tell me that you lost your phone."

"It's actually a funny story," I say, knowing that she won't find it the least bit funny. "But I've really got to—"

"I know, I know. Thanks for calling, Will. I'm so glad to hear your voice."

And we say good-bye.

We are still inside Dairy Queen. My father seems stumped, irritated.

"Does anything at all look familiar to you?"

I ask Maria Rosa. "From when you were here before. The mountains? The river? Beaverhead Rock? Anything?"

Her brown eyes stare back blankly. She shrugs.

My father interjects from across the table, "You've never been here before, have you?"

Maria looks at him, expressionless. Those same brown eyes that tell us nothing. A face that keeps its secrets.

He waits for an answer.

She finally surrenders a shake of the head, no.

"Does your cousin expect you? Does he even know that you are in the country?" he asks.

I watch her closely. She swallows, looks down. "*Lo siento*," she whispers softly.

She is sorry.

"There *is* a cousin, right?"

"Oh, *sí, sí*," Maria says. Once again she pulls out the folded and refolded index card. "Alejandro," she says, tapping it on the table with an index finger.

Unfortunately, we've already visited that address. It brought us to a small downtown apartment

building. There was no Alejandro. We asked around. No one seemed to remember him—or if they did, they would not say.

My father nods, chews on a fry, looks at me thoughtfully. "What would Meriwether Lewis do in this situation, Will? Do you think he'd give up? Go home? Forget about it?"

"He wouldn't give up," I say.

"What about you?" he asks.

"We have to keep trying. We can't just . . ." My voice trails off.

A policeman enters, glances our way, and moves to the counter. I watch Maria shrink in her seat. "Let me tell you a story," my father says. His eyes shift to check the cop, he leans forward, and begins.

On August 12, 1805, Captain Lewis got his first clear view of the Rocky Mountains. He climbed to the peak of the Lemhi Pass, right at the Continental Divide, and he saw what was still ahead. He was staggered by the reality of their immense size and scope, range after range after

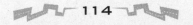

range without end. That's when he knew they were in deep trouble. This was not like the modest mountains that Lewis knew from back east. I try to imagine how he must have felt right at that moment. Up until that time, they had all hoped that it would be an easy hike. A day, maybe two, possibly even lugging canoes. Nobody knew exactly what they'd have to deal with until that moment when Lewis climbed the ridge and saw how far they still had to go—the snow-capped mountain range—and how incredibly difficult it would be. They had already traveled more than three thousand miles. His men had been through so much. The worst was yet to come.

A normal person might have wanted to give up. But not Lewis. He knew he might die in those terrible mountains, but he was prepared to go all the way. That's courage. To keep going.

Running out of time and ideas, we pull into a gas station on the edge of town. The air is hot and muggy. My father fills the tank, one arm propped against the

side of the car. He looks spent and discouraged. I grab Paco's leash and take him out for a sniff around. The mosquitoes descend like dive-bombers, darting all around me. I smack one, then another, as they land on my neck and arm.

Maria Rosa waits in the car.

"Need anything inside?" my father calls. He returns the nozzle to the pump. There's a small store inside the gas station.

"I'm good," I say.

I notice a young man, dark like Maria Rosa, leaning against the building. He wears a blue button-down shirt and jeans. A red rag hangs from his pocket. A mechanic, probably. And I know in that instant: *It's him*. Alejandro. I can't explain how I know this is true, but the jolt is like lightning. When I was little I used to drag my stocking feet across our living room carpet, then I'd go up to my mother and shock her with my finger. That's how I felt when I saw Alejandro. Zapped!

I knock on the passenger window. "Maria? Maria Rosa?"

She looks up at me in confusion through the glass. I point, "Look," and her head slowly swivels. In that instant, the car door swings open, and everything changes, no more, forever.

We pull the car off to a parking spot in the shade. We are giving them time, according to my father. He waits beneath a tree, leaning back on his hands. I wander off a little ways, throwing rocks, missing targets. Maria is sorting it out with the cousin, we hope. And we also hope it will all be okay.

Soon after, Maria comes to me. "He says," she sobs, "he says—" She sobs some more, gasping for air.

"What is it?" I ask. "What did he say?"

"He says, 'No Paco,'" Maria cries. Tears well up and tumble down her cheeks. She collapses to the ground and wraps her arms around the dog.

I am furious, and my anger makes me fearless. I march up to Alejandro, who stands arms crossed by the garage door. His hair is black and slicked back. He wears a tattoo of a wild horse on his neck; a cigarette dangles from his lip.

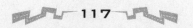

"How can you be so mean?" I say. "That dog is everything to her."

Alejandro takes a slow drag of his cigarette, flicks it to the ground, crushes it with his boot. He raises his hands in the air, palms up, a gesture of helplessness. "What can I do? The landlord's rules. No pets."

There's a sly grin on his face. None of this makes him terribly unhappy. Out of the corner of my eye, I see my father watching us. He sees Maria Rosa wailing, leaning heavily against Paco, and starts toward her.

"You can ask," I say. "You can move to a new apartment. You can—"

"I will take my little cousin into my home," he tells me. "I will help her find work. She is my family. But no dogs. No." He slices his hand sharply crosswise, palm down. "Besides, I cannot afford to feed a huge animal like that."

"But . . . ?" I sputter helplessly. *What can I say that will change his mind?* "We can give you money for food. My father—"

"What business is it of yours?" Alejandro sniffs.

He points to Paco. "You take the dog, you love it so much."

And that is how the notion first came to us. After much discussion, we agree to return in less than a week on our way back to retrieve Paco. "What about Mom?" I ask doubtfully.

My father draws his lips into a thin line. "If it's a problem, I'll take Paco."

I'm thrilled. To my surprise, Maria sees the sense of it. Shrugging, she accepts life's hard bargain. Before we leave, I rummage in my backpack, find a postcard, and scribble my address and phone number on the back of it. I find Maria inside the service area, seated on a tire, watching Alejandro work on an engine. She is sipping a Coke, Paco beside her, a clear plastic bowl filled with water between his forepaws.

"I wanted you to have this," I say, handing her the card. "You can call me, anytime."

She opens her arms, and I fall into her grateful embrace. She surprises me with a kiss, warm lips pressed to my forehead.

"Sweet," she whispers.

Alejandro, leaning into the engine, leers over his shoulder. "She thinks you're a sweet little boy."

Maria Rosa squeezes my hand.

"We'll be back for Paco," I promise, stooping to scratch the dog's thick neck and head. And so I say good-bye—but not good-bye forever, not yet—to a fifteen-year-old girl named Maria Rosa, who I met wandering lost on the Lewis and Clark Trail.

Pretty amazing, right? The photo on the front is of the Lemhi Pass and I imagine that it hasn't changed much from when Lewis & Clark came here 200 years ago. Believe it. Sometimes I can squeeze my eyes and imagine what it must have felt like—to see this incredible place for the first time— America! Home! Other days, I miss McNuggets. Ha-ha. Kidding!

It is quiet in the car as we head west on 324. We both feel the absence of Maria and Paco. We left them behind, yet they linger in my thoughts. Was it wrong,

I wonder, to help a girl who is possibly in this country illegally? It is a puzzle I can't piece together. I turn to look back down the disappearing road.

"We'll see her again," my father says, as if reading my emotions. "When we come to pick up Paco on our way home. That way we'll make sure she's okay."

I still feel unsettled.

"We can only do what we think is right," he says.

The late afternoon has turned bright and clear, as if a page had been turned in a child's picture book. We are still on the trail.

My father points to Clark Canyon Dam. "Obviously, that cement monstrosity wasn't here when they came through. This whole country went dam happy in the fifties. There are places where the expedition stayed, Camp Fortunate for starters, that are now underwater. The spawning salmon never had a chance. Even today, when it's time to run, some of them are still bumping their heads into cement walls." I look out the window and try to imagine a past buried by water. All the footprints erased. My father is still trying to tell me things, always the teacher, though I don't know why it's so important to him.

We turn onto a narrow gravel road, up and up, to the Lemhi Pass. Here the landscape feels remote and untouched, except for power lines and picnic areas, random road signs and cars. It is as if I were seeing the same world that they saw. It connects us across time. My father finds a place near the summit to pull over. A sign tells us that we are more than seven thousand feet above sea level, the highest elevation on the Lewis and Clark Trail.

We stop to admire the view. There are open slopes for as far as I can see, with rugged mountains to the west. There have been times on our trip, speeding down some highway, when I haven't been able to imagine what it was like in the old days before everything changed. But up here, in this spot, I can feel it in my bones. Like the song goes, "This land is my land . . ."

I ask, "How could anyone hike across it?"

"That's surely what Captain Lewis wondered," my

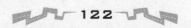

father replies. "Lewis stood somewhere close to this spot. He looked at those mountains—remember, no white American had actually seen the Rockies up close before—and he knew without a doubt that unless they had horses to help carry their load, they'd all die, wandering in that maze of bare rock and stone. To make matters worse, he's trying to find a tribe, the Shoshones, who prefer to stay hidden. They are poor, lack guns, and are fearful of rival tribes, the Blackfeet in particular. Lewis has heard stories from French trappers and other tribes that the Shoshones had horses. Maybe they can strike a trade. If—*if!*—he can find them! Somehow Lewis has got to figure out a way to make friends with those Indians and get them to sell him at least twenty-five horses. Plus, he really needs a guide. Except for a few trinkets—beads and mirrors and cheap scissors—he's basically got nothing left to trade. Will, he's facing absolute disaster! If Lewis can't find horses—and fast, like immediately—then the expedition is doomed. They will have to turn around and go home. The entire mission a failure."

My father stands there, staring to the west, eyes wide and gesturing. I have to laugh at his wiry energy. "So what happened?" I ask.

"What happened? Basically, he got lucky," my father says. "He got very lucky."

"Tell me," I say, because I want to know.

"You sure I'm not boring you?" he teases.

"Dad, just—"

"Okay," he says, "I'm glad you're interested for a change."

"Dad," I protest.

"I'm not complaining," he says. "So, anyway, Lewis makes an important decision. He grabs three men—Drouillard, Shields, and McNeal—and leaves the group behind. Lewis takes off to search for the Shoshones, come hell or high water."

"Mom says that," I interrupt.

"Yes, she sure does," my father says, smiling. "It's a very old expression. In fact, Lewis used it in his journals more than two hundred years ago. Here's the thing about Lewis. As a rule, he believes the road ahead is good unless proven otherwise."

"What do you mean?" I ask.

"Positive thinking," my father says. "That's another lesson from old Meriwether. He's come a long way. He's not turning back now, no way, no how. Courage keeps walking."

The light dwindles, the day fades to dusk. It's past time we make camp. We return to the car and roll down a semi-terrifying, one-lane road—narrow and steep, with wicked, sharp turns—and we find an old campsite off Agency Creek Road. It doesn't look like anybody's ever been to this site, though I know that's unlikely.

After a simple dinner of mac and cheese and some energy bars, we sit and stare into the fire, the same way folks gaze endlessly into flickering computer screens.

A breeze picks up, swirling round us. I lean back on my hands and tilt my head back to look at the high treetops. They sway in the wind, bending with the air currents, like graceful dancers. The rustling leaves whisper a magical language, changing with the breeze from dark to light and back again. Sparks from the fire rise and whirl and die. Did Meriwether Lewis sit in this very spot and feel this same sense of wonder?

"This is nice," I hear myself say. I don't remember thinking it. The words just spill out.

"Yeah, it's beautiful," he replies. "It's maybe my favorite place on the planet."

"No, not that," I say. "This, us. Being here with you. I like it."

My father doesn't speak, just reaches for a stick, tosses it into the fire. "I'm sorry," he says, and gets up awkwardly, brushing furiously at the dirt on his pants. No more words between us tonight, but somehow, for once, we've managed to say enough. Or at least, I hope so.

I place another log on the fire. Listening to my father talk that night—of Lewis alone, of Lewis laying down his rifle before the arrival of sixty Shoshone warriors riding bareback on horses, of warm greetings and a shared smoke and an invitation back to camp—I saw a spark in my father

that I hadn't seen in a long time. He was alive inside the drama of the story. The firelight danced, his hands moved and formed shadows, and the stars were so close I felt as if I could reach out and touch them.

FUN FACT: There's a vertical line that runs through the entire United States called the Continental Divide. It's like a spine. To the east of it, the rivers roll through the plains to the Gulf of Mexico. To the west, everything goes the other way, toward the Pacific Ocean. Today I lay down across it, my feet in the east, my head in the west. Because, you know, I'm amazing that way!

I awake that night with a start in the pulsing dark of the tent. *Something isn't right*, a voice whispers inside my head. I fall back into a black, dreamless sleep, not awake long enough to even wonder what it might be.

The most
terrible mountains
I ever
beheld.

—PATRICK GASS, SOLDIER,

CORPS OF DISCOVERY

CHAPTER FOUR

THE TERRIBLE MOUNTAINS

We wake to the sounds of the same birdsongs that Captain Lewis must have heard. I take an experimental sip of my father's coffee, which is totally disgusting. Hot chocolate is the drink for me. Soon we are driving a thirty-seven-mile, scenic loop road and then we head back north. Can someone get bored with nonstop amazing sights? I'm voting yes. Still, we saw two moose—mooses? mice?—and that was extremely cool.

We have to "resupply," as my father calls it, before we head out for a three-day hike on the Lolo Trail.

To my father, that means a stop into town for food and gear. To me, it means one thing: bear spray.

"I don't know that we need that," Dad says inside the camp store. "It's a well-traveled trail."

"I do," I say, holding the canister. "This is exactly what we need."

Gently, he says, "It's not like mosquito repellent, Will. Do you even know how it works?"

I am, by now, the world's foremost expert on exactly how it works. I have read the label and the packaging from start to finish—twice. I've nearly memorized it.

"Please," I say.

"Well, maybe you're right," he says, placing the spray into the basket. "Let's hope we don't have to use it."

"It comes with a hip holster," I point out, "and shoots up to thirty feet."

"That's nice," my father says, "but a grizzly can cover a hundred yards in six seconds."

If a bear charges toward you, you spray a cloud of pure nasty that keeps the bear away. If it's raining

or windy that day, then you might be out of luck. If the bear keeps coming, you hit it with another blast of spray. And if it still keeps coming? Curl up in a ball and kiss your butt good-bye.

I have a bad feeling about our hike through the Bitterroot Range. Plus, I heard two guys talking about mountain lions, as if I don't have enough to worry about. My dad, however, seems especially gung-ho. At least if I'm going to face a bear, I'll have pepper spray.

When the Corps of Discovery met up with the Shoshones, it was a happy time for the entire expedition. Especially for Sacagawea, who was shocked to be reunited with her brother, Chief Cameahwait, whom she thought she'd never see again. You might say she was pretty surprised to see him, and it was definitely good news for the Corps. The Shoshones agreed to sell horses, as well as provide the Corps with a guide, Old Toby, to take them through the Bitterroots. The dream of an easy water passage to the Pacific had died.

They would have to hump it over those harsh mountains. The Corps set out on September 1, 1805. The hike was long and brutal, a three-week slog through rugged wilderness. Packhorses slipped and fell and crashed down ravines. The expedition crossed open meadows, climbed steep and stony slopes, followed creeks between narrow mountain gaps—all with little food to eat. Often the path was overgrown by thickets and fallen trees. The weather grew colder. It rained. It froze. It snowed. The men became lost, exhausted, and very, very hungry.

The next few days should be tough. This will be my first time doing true backcountry hiking. There are no stores, no cozy hotels. We are carrying everything on our backs—food, sleeping bag, tent, clothes, and, oh yes, bear spray. This isn't pulling the car into a campsite and hauling out a cooler and pillows from the trunk. For this section of the Lolo Trail, we're leaving the car behind; we'll get a ride back later on down the trail.

Ugh. I heave the bulky pack onto my back and immediately sag under the increased heft. Tighten the belt around my hips, adjust the shoulder straps so that it sits snugly against my back. There's water within reach in my side pocket, and the spray sits easily in the holster.

"Let's ramble," my father says.

"*Ramble*? Really?"

"It's an old expression that Lewis used," he explains. "I guess a lot of folks did, back in those times."

I miss Ollie and Maria Rosa. Now it's just us, me and my dad. We start to walk, west along the ridge, along a dirt trail. The day is young. I feel steady and strong. So far.

"Lewis in particular loved to roam and explore," my father says. "Clark was more of a river man, the one to keep the expedition functioning and moving forward. Meanwhile, Lewis would get out of the boat and walk—sometimes twenty, thirty miles in a single day."

I hear his voice behind me, drifting over my head

like wind in my sails. Normally it might drive me a little crazy, but out here I'm glad for the words to keep me company. "Lewis would stop and look at things. Take notes, draw pictures. He was a botanist, a great noticer of things. I feel sorry for your generation, Will. Kids today miss the freedom to explore on their own."

"It's not our fault," I point out. "We'd love to be free. Parents won't let us."

"The world has changed," my father says, and I can hear him sigh. "Not for the better."

"Old people always say that, but it's not true," I argue. "Everybody talks about the good old days . . . when there was slavery and diseases wiped out entire tribes and nobody had indoor plumbing."

My father hoots. "You would have missed the toilets, huh?"

"Oh yeah," I shoot back over my shoulder, laughing. "If nothing else, this trip has made me really appreciate toilets."

We pause often to drink water, chomp on trail mix, but mostly to unshoulder the packs. Each time,

though, it gets harder for me to mule it back on again. After a couple of hours, a sign lets us know that we've crossed into Idaho.

We've been silent for a long while. Every once in a while I sing out, or clap my hands, to make sure we don't startle a bear that might be around the corner. That's the worst thing you can do, they say—surprise a bear. The guy working the cash register at the store explained that bears don't want to see us any more than we want to see them. "If they hear you coming," he told me, "they'll make themselves scarce."

I sing a lot, though it's sad how few lyrics I actually know. My father has already requested that I not sing "The Wheels on the Bus" ever, ever again. Can't say I blame him. After a while, my focus shifts from the possibility of bear attacks to my sore legs and aching feet.

Are we having fun yet?

I think of Maria Rosa and wonder about my mother.

I know what my father is doing. He wants me to

"experience the hardship" of the original expedition. He thinks I have it too easy. That I'm not tough enough. Well, great, I get it; the original expedition wasn't easy. Now let's get back in the car and eat cookies.

A question pops into my mind. "Who do you think would win in a fight—a grizzly or a lowland gorilla?"

My father laughs. "What is this, one of those Batman versus Spider-Man debates?"

"Seriously," I say, pausing to shift the pack on my shoulders. I fail to find a comfortable spot.

"Well, in the first place, it would never happen. Gorillas live in tropical—"

"Oh, come on," I protest. "Just imagine that it could happen. Which animal do you think would win?"

"All right, I'll play. Let's analyze it." He pauses, reaches to my side pocket, pulls out the water bottle, and tells me to stay hydrated. "Now, some of my facts may be a little off since Wi-Fi is spotty out here at best."

He pulls out his phone, frowns, and pockets it.

"I'd estimate that a male grizzly weighs from five to eight hundred pounds. A male lowland gorilla weighs about three fifty. That's a huge difference right there."

"Yeah, but gorillas are seriously, insanely strong. They can swing huge sticks and jump around."

My father ignores this. "Both have large canine teeth. A bear has long claws, while a gorilla only has nails."

For some reason, I find myself rooting for the gentle gorilla. "Gorillas are smart," I note. "And agile."

"Bears are carnivores," he counters. "They have the kill instinct. In fights, bears go for the neck. They've been known to kill moose. I don't think there are many reports of gorillas making that kind of lethal attack."

"How do you even know this stuff?" I ask.

My father shrugs, and then it dawns on me. "You've thought about this before!"

"Yes, I suppose I have. Don't all boys? Maybe you and I have something in common after all. You're a boy, and I used to be one."

We hoist the packs back on our shoulders. "I'm

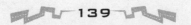

sorry I brought it up," I admit. "It's depressing to think about."

"You're right," my father agrees. "I only wish we lived in a world where gorillas and bears could just get along!" We take a few strides and he says, "Now when it comes to Batman versus Spider-Man—"

"Oh, that's an easy one!" I exclaim.

And that's how we pass our time on the Lolo Trail, talking pure nonsense, thinking weird thoughts, singing bad songs, and every once in a while stopping in our tracks, looking around, and saying, "Holy wow, this might be the most beautiful place on Earth."

We are walking, walking, walking. The backpack slices into my shoulders, cuts into my hip. I'm pretty sure I've got a small, sharp rock in my right hiking boot. Tiny bugs I can't identify are chomping on my hands, face, and neck. "Let me tell you a story," my father begins, and I zone out.

The scenery is amazing, for sure. We'll hike on a path with trees on each side of us, then we'll come to a rise, the land will open up before us, and we can see for miles into the distance. But most of the time I'm staring at the ground, putting one foot in front of the other. I'm relieved when my father says, "Okay, hold your horses. We'll camp here."

We set up camp, quickly and without conversation. We're getting good at it, and we're too bone-tired to talk. I pull off my boots and socks. *Ouch.* My feet are blistered and sore. Even worse, when I complain, my father tells me to let them breathe, he'll patch me up later with pieces of moleskin. "Get some rest," he suggests. "Read something."

I explain that I left my book back in the car. Too heavy to lug around, I figured. He says to look in the bottom pocket of his pack, there's a book in there. Groaning, I find a book about—you guessed it!—Lewis and Clark. It's all he ever thinks about. Normally I'd reach for a graphic novel if I had a choice, but I forgot my library card. I'm stuck with what my dad brought. Yet after a few minutes flipping the pages, I'm sucked into the book because it's filled with photographs and cool pictures. There are even photos of things I recognize. Places I've seen. Fort Mandan. The White Cliffs. The Lemhi Pass.

And there are places I want to see, most especially the white-water rapids of the Lochsa River. I definitely want a chance to experience that. It looks like a blast. There are a lot of old photographs of Native people. Not the specific Indians that the Corps met along the trail, of course—they are all dead now—but people from the same tribes. I guess the Native people were confused by it all, not quite sure what to make of those white wanderers bearing gifts and guns, telling tales of their "new father" in the east.

I come across a reproduction of a painting. I call to my father, "Hey, Dad, who's the black guy?"

He glances over; I hold the book up to show him the picture.

"That's York, Clark's slave. He came along on the trip."

I take this in for a moment. I don't know why I hadn't noticed it before. They actually brought a slave across the entire country. And somehow that's not totally creepy?

"They dragged him along, like you dragged me," I say.

"Hardly," my father scoffs. "You're just another

spoiled kid who watches too much television. York was a real slave. William Clark owned him. They grew up together."

Chill, Dad, I was joking. I know I'm not actually a slave.

"Wherever the expedition traveled, the Native people were amazed by York, who by all reports was very large and muscular," my father the professor can't help but explain. "They'd never seen a black man before. On at least one occasion, the Native people rubbed dirt on his skin to try to make it come off."

"So did Clark let him go free after the trip?" I ask.

"No, things got even worse," my father says. "After they returned, York argued for his freedom. He said, in essence, 'Look, I traveled as an equal with all of you for two and half years. We hunted, hauled, and faced many dangers together. Every man was paid money and given land. All except for me. I got nothing. So in payment, I ask you, please set me free.'"

I waited. "And?"

"He got bupkis."

"Bupkis?" I asked.

"It's a Yiddish word. It means 'nothing.' Clark

wouldn't do it. He refused to grant York his freedom. In fact, in later years Clark became quite unhappy with York, whom he considered impudent."

Impudent? Dad! Speak English!

"It means 'not showing due respect,'" my father explains. He sighs, runs a hand across his jaw. "Times were different back then."

"I guess so," I say, thinking about how much changes, and how much seems to stay the same.

Later that same night, I'm humming to myself, bone tired, lying on top of my sleeping bag, leafing through the book I borrowed from my father. I turn the page to discover an envelope tucked between the pages like a dried wildflower. It's already been torn open. The return address is from a woman at the University of Oregon in Eugene. Jan Carr. Curious, I read it, though I know the letter was not intended for my eyes.

I am surprised when I feel tightness in my chest and it's harder to breathe and when the paper in my hands won't hold still. I seriously didn't know I cared that much. My father has been invited to visit as a guest lecturer. The letter requests a meeting, a dinner, an intimate gathering—with this Jan woman. She wants to discuss my father's interest in a new position as head of the history department.

It suddenly all makes sense.

That's what this trip is all about.

My father is leaving me.

Leaving me for the second time.

The liar, the fake. The man who leaves. He's not trying to spend more time with me. He's saying good-bye.

During their last desperate days on the Lolo Trail, the men grew weak and ill. The supply of food was gone. The easy hunting of the massive buffalo herds was long behind them. The large animals had fled down to the meadows and plains. There was little game to kill, except for an occasional squirrel or pheasant. The weather turned bad. It rained, and they were pelted by sleet and hail. One morning, the travelers awoke

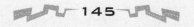

to three inches of snow. It continued to snow all that day. The Corps were forced to kill a colt to eat. The next day (I'm sorry, I know this is gross!), they used snow and what was left of the horse to make colt soup. Some of the men grew very sick.

Still, they refused to give up. Lewis and Clark even took the risk of splitting into two groups, to better their chances of finding food. They killed and ate another horse. Finally, after three weeks of wandering in the wilderness, Clark and his men arrived at a village of the Nez Perce people in the Weippe Prairie. Captain Lewis followed soon after. The men were sick and weary. They hoped the Indians would be kind.

We continue to slog along the Lolo Trail, but I am so done. My father tries to talk to me. I don't reply. I don't even listen. Because I now understand what this trip was all about. Something was wrong from the beginning. For the longest time I couldn't figure it out. But now I know.

I know a kid named Justin St. Pierre. Fancy name,

right? He's not really a friend, actually. But, anyway. Justin's parents are divorced, and his father moved away, got remarried, and started a new family. He's got two little boys who Justin calls his "half brothers." Justin brags about his father a little too much, like he's trying to convince himself, so I know it has to hurt. Here's the thing that gets me. Every year, his father whisks Justin off for an amazing vacation. Disneyland, Legoland, even the Wizarding World of Harry Potter. Awesome, right? Who wouldn't love that? For one week, Mr. St. Pierre becomes the World's Greatest Dad!

Justin waits for those trips all year.

But then what happens? Justin gets plopped home for another year and doesn't hear from the World's Greatest Dad except for birthday cards, text messages, and random phone calls. Meanwhile, the WGD is far away, enjoying his new and improved family. I seriously think that's what this trip on the Lewis and Clark Trail has been all about. I've become Justin St. Pierre . . . and this is my crummy week in Disneyland.

It's a small world after all.

Back before we started, my father brought me to Denny's because he knows it's my weakness. He said he needed me—needed my eyes, to see the land for the first time—and now I'm calling baloney. He never brought me on his trips before. He always said that I'd probably hate it.

Well, he was right.

I *do* hate it.

I literally, totally do.

And right now, this minute, I hate him.

I know his secret. He's leaving to take a job in Oregon. I wonder when he's going to find the courage to tell me.

You know that expression "I'm so hungry I could eat a horse!"? Well, there were times on the expedition in the Bitterroot Mountains—where we're at right now as I write this!—that the guys really were that hungry, and they really did eat a horse. More than once. Burp. And you thought hot dogs were bad!

I'm tired, I'm sort of freaked, and so maybe I throw a water bottle at my father. I know, not cool, but I'm not at my best today. I just fell and banged my knee something wicked. It's all scratched up, and I'm bleeding down to my sock. My dad is full of advice and I don't want to hear it, thank you very much, so I launch the water bottle in his direction. Splashes him pretty good, too.

"I don't want to do this anymore," I say.

"Will," my father says in a measured voice, "you're tired. Maybe we're trying to do too much—"

"I know your secret," I snap. "I found the letter."

I wildly sling the backpack over my shoulder, and it throws me off balance.

"What are you talking about?" he says, acting wide-eyed and surprised. But he can't fool me. I see the worry in his eyes.

The next second, I break into a run, or sort of one, as fast as I can go with a massive backpack weighing me down. It's more of a cross between a hurried walk and a slow jog. My stupid, injured knee kills with each step. Doesn't matter. I'm moving as quickly as I can, creating distance between my father and me.

This time, *I'm* leaving *him.*

"Will, hold up, hold up," my father calls. "You dropped—"

But I'm so mad, I'm not listening anymore.

I'm down the path, around the bend. My heart is hammering. I am blind with rage, deaf to his cries.

Five minutes later, I turn a bend and see a bear cub on the path, about thirty yards away. It looks up at me, curious. My heart climbs into my throat. I stand there, motionless, and try to remember how to exhale.

A bear cub is the worst possible thing anyone can find on a remote mountain trail. There's movement in the thicket up ahead. Something big coming through, branches snapping under the weight. A black nose pokes through. Followed by the massive head and shoulders of the wildest, most dangerous beast I've ever seen.

Out for a ramble one fair June day, Lewis scouted the Great Falls of the Missouri River. He carried only his rifle and espontoon, a sort of spear that

150

doubled as a walking stick, which he used as a prop to steady his rifle for a long shot. Meriwether Lewis came across a herd of buffalo and shot one through the lungs. As the dying animal spurted blood through its mouth and nostrils, Lewis failed to immediately reload his rifle. Big mistake. Reloading took precious time, even for a practiced hunter like Lewis. Just then a grizzly appeared and began to advance upon Lewis. There was nowhere to hide. No trees, no thickets. Lewis turned and began to walk quickly toward the river. The bear followed briskly behind him, gaining. Lewis broke into a run and leaped into the river. When he got into waist-deep water, Lewis turned to face the oncoming bear. He held out his spear-like espontoon, hoping to fend off the grizzly in the water. The bear paused, uncertain about this new creature, and wheeled away without attacking. It didn't want to fight in the water. Lewis was saved. From that day on, he vowed to never again leave his rifle unloaded.

For a moment that seems to last an eternity, there is no movement on the trail. I am inside a photograph, a picture postcard, frozen in time. Two bears and a boy. *Snap*, the shutter clicks.

The cub sits on the path, near a patch of yellow wildflowers. Close enough that I could hit it with a rock. The big bear, the mother, takes a position to the side and in front of her cub. She is solid black, not a grizzly after all, but the smaller, more aggressive species of black bear.

She comes toward me, a step and another, and rises threateningly on her rear legs. A horrible cry roars from her throat and lungs. Down she stomps, up and down, and again, falling like thunder. She pops her jaws and swats at the ground, blowing and snorting through her nose.

If she is making this display to terrify me, it's working. I do not move because I cannot move. I am too filled with shock to think straight. My mind sputters and misfires as I try to manage the fear that overwhelms me. I can smell it, an odor I'll never forget, strong and rank and bitter. It is the aroma of

death. I remember something—a piece of advice—
never stare directly at a bear because it will be per-
ceived as a threat. I avert my gaze, look to the
ground.

I wish to make myself invisible. To disappear.
To vanish into thin air.

I know I can't run—it will be an invitation for
attack. I slowly reach my right hand to my hip
holster. It's empty. The spray canister isn't there. I
remember my father calling after me, *Will, hold up,
hold up. You dropped—*

The bear spray.

That's what he was trying to tell me.

It must have fallen off back on the trail.

The bear again roars and moves menacingly forward. Should I lie down? Should I scream? Is there
time for me to climb a tree? I don't know what to do,
and so instead I do nothing.

"Will," my father says, beckoning in an urgent
whisper.

He has followed me up the trail. I turn and
see him, cautiously hanging back, crouched low.

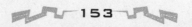

He waves the bear spray can in a slow movement. I instinctively take a step toward him.

"Stay calm, Will," he says in a soft voice. "Easy, easy. We'll get you out of this. Don't move."

The bear begins to pace, back and forth, back and forth. Hostile, agitated, nervous: teeth bared, snorting, on the verge of attack. She checks her cub, steps toward it, growls, and whirls again to face me.

When my father steps closer, the bear growls again, as if to warn, *Not another step.*

"That's okay," my father speaks directly to the animal. "We're not here to hurt you, bear. No, no, no." Then to me he says, "That's good, Will. You are doing fine. The bear is as frightened as you are, believe me. Now very slowly, very carefully, without turning, take a small step toward me."

My feet don't move.

My knees and legs begin to move, jittering up and down like the needle of my mom's sewing machine. I'm shivering, trembling, suddenly cold all over.

"Okay, um, we'll try this instead," my father says. "I want you to slowly, slowly take off the pack. Can

you do that, Will? You are just going to leave it right there."

Somehow I am able to unbuckle the waist strap and quietly, gently, shrug the pack off my shoulders. I lower it to the ground as carefully as if it were a newborn baby.

My father says, "Now I'm going to throw the spray can to you." He pauses. "Do you hear me, Will?"

I am aware that he's talking to me, asking me a question. He wants an answer, a nod, something, anything. But my tongue fails me; it feels like a swollen kitchen sponge has been stuffed into my mouth. I make no reply, only stare and stare.

"Watch me, Will. Do you see? Get ready," my father says in a soft, soothing voice. He steps forward like a bowler, bent low, arcing the spray can high into the air with an underhand toss. I watch helplessly as it sails far over my head, missing its mark by ten feet. My father never could throw. The spray can bangs against a rock with an abrupt clatter and tumbles, bouncing and rolling, toward the bears. This sudden,

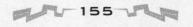

unexpected movement alarms the cub. It lets out a muffled noise, like the sound a plush toy makes when you squeeze its belly. The young cub pivots, stumbling and tumbling in its haste, and hurries off down the trail. The great black mother turns, too, hesitates for a long moment, offers one final look in our direction, and retreats after her cub. My spirit animal melts into the wilderness, leaving us alone on the trail once more.

Slowly, my scattered brain reassembles. It recovers its ability to send messages to my feet. I walk toward my father, barely able to lift my boots off the ground. He comes swiftly to me, arms open, and we hug tightly. He's speaking to me, whispering how he loves me, how I'm safe now, how the bear has gone away. "Let's go," he says into my ear, tugging me, his arm wrapped around my neck. He bends to grab the loop strap of my pack and carries it like a child in both arms. I stagger forward, still dazed. My senses slowly return: sight, smell, hearing. And so we head back in the opposite direction. These will be the last steps I take on the Lolo Trail. Moving the wrong way.

Even then, in that fog, I understand the bear was only being a bear. True to its nature.

I know that.

I also know that I failed the courage test.

We hike in long, quick strides without pause for ten minutes, side by side, really moving. "Don't look back," my father advises, while looking back himself. The path is narrow here, crowded by trees on both sides. I catch him glancing at me, too, watchful. Finally our path opens up, and we can see for miles. It's as if the sky has weight and drops down on our heads. He signals for us to stop. Ahead there's a side trail to the left that connects with the Lolo Motorway, a nearby forest road. When we reach it, we walk east. It's hardly a road at all. When a car passes my father turns and, beseechingly, sticks out his thumb. *Whoosh*. It doesn't even slow down. We get a ride not long after from an old Idaho cowboy in a Ford pickup truck. He's got the hat and the mustache and everything. We throw our gear into the back and squeeze three across into the front. His name is Earl, he tells us, and a toothpick dangles precariously from his lips the entire drive—not a great distance, actually, back to Highway 12 where we parked our car.

Earl and my father make small talk, about the trail mostly, the history around these parts, and the return of the wolves from Canada. I sit looking out the windshield, but I might as well have had my eyes sewn closed. I don't see a thing.

The car is waiting for us, locked tight, Dad's gray Subaru Forester. Now we turn back west, and the road drops down along the Lochsa River. I don't ask where we're going. We sit mostly in silence, the river to our left. It's been a long, long day. A wooden sign announces that we've entered the town of Lowell. My father puts on the blinker when we come to a big red sign that reads, THREE RIVERS MOTEL: COCKTAILS, WI-FI, POOL.

My father offers a joke: "Looks like they've got all the major food groups covered."

On another day, I might have laughed.

He checks his phone. No service. We're still in the middle of nowhere, but, yes, it is a beautiful spot.

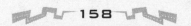

Good old, weird America. He rents a simple motel room—the TV has only four channels—but it has a tub and shower and two beds.

Still, as tired as we are, the river calls to us. We head down to it, a place where soon the Lochsa meets the Selway and becomes the Clearwater. It will eventually flow into the Columbia and feed into the Pacific Ocean.

There we sit, sharing a bag of Doritos. I feel hollow inside. Still freaked, I guess. My father senses it, I suppose, and says, "You did good back there, Will."

I glance at him, shake my head. I know that I did nothing at all. If that bear charged me, I don't believe I would have moved a muscle.

He says, "I've read all the articles and talked to a lot of experienced backpackers, Will, and nobody can agree on the right way to react during a bear encounter. There are a lot of opinions. Each bear and each situation is different."

"I just stood there," I say, barely able to push my voice past my lips.

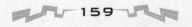

"And maybe that was the best thing in that situation," he suggests.

I shrug, unconvinced. "I dropped the bear spray, like an idiot. I was mad at you, and I ran down the trail with my head down, not thinking."

My father nods, smart enough not to disagree.

I remember, now, why I was upset, why I took off alone down that trail. There seems no good way to say it. "I know you're leaving, Dad," I blurt, "and if you have to go—"

"What's that, Will?" My father tilts his head, lips pursed, genuinely confused.

"I saw the letter," I say. "In your book."

He picks at a bite on his arm. "Will, honestly, I still don't know—"

"The job in Oregon," I prod.

The lightbulb goes off. My father shakes his head, runs a hand across his jaw. "There's no job in Oregon, Will. I mean, there's a conference and I might give a lecture, but . . ." He pauses, leans back, as if seeing me for the first time in a long time.

"What's this about, son?"

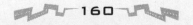

The river before us rumbles to the sea. It refuses to linger and seems rowdier than the Missouri, narrow and swift, roaring down from the high peaks. Now I am the one who is confused. "If you aren't going away, then why'd you take me on this trip?"

"It was your mother's idea," he confesses. "She wanted us to spend time together." There's something odd in his voice, a choked quality that sucks the shimmer from the sky. A darkening gathers all around us. Dusk on the river. Even the birds stop to listen.

He's not going anywhere.

"That makes no sense," I say.

"Will, your mom . . ." His voice cracks. He shuts his mouth, looks away.

"What?" I insist.

"I don't—" he begins, then stops. My father brings his arm around my shoulders, pulls me close. "She's sick, Will. That's why we're on this trip, the both of us together. This is what she asked me to do."

"I talked to her just the other day. She said she had

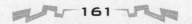

a cold," I argue. But I know it even as I talk—I know it in my bones—he's not talking about a cold.

She's sick, he said.

His left hand reaches over and becomes so entangled with my own fingers I can barely tell where one hand ends and the other begins. He says that everything is going to be okay. That this is the most important thing for me to know. It will all be okay.

Listening to him, I doubt that he believes it himself, but I nod. My lips might even form the words: *I know it*. I still have no idea what he's talking about, other than the sorrowful feeling behind his words. Their grave weight.

"The doctors found something," he explains. "A small tumor. In her breast." His hand goes to his chest, as if probing for his heart.

Then he says it, the word no one wants to hear: "Cancer."

It frightens me to see him so shaken, so unsure of himself. He's scared, too, I realize.

"We should be with her," I say.

He nods again, tight-lipped, thinking. "Aunt

Barbara is staying with your mom now. Right or wrong, I think your mother needed time to tackle this on her own, begin the treatment, sort of get a handle on things. She's worried about you."

"Me?"

"She's a mother," he says. "Like that bear on the trail."

This feels scarier than any bear.

"It wasn't the perfect plan, to tell you this way," he admits, "but it's not a perfect world." He leans into me. I feel his weight against my side. "It *is* scary. But your mom is strong, Will. The doctors found it early. That's important, and it's good. We can handle this. Together. Things aren't going to change. None of this is your fault."

I think of Ollie back at Judith Landing. He hugged my father and said, *You've got this.* I realize now that he must have known already. Maybe that's why he met up with us on the river. It was planned.

"Ollie knew," I said.

"Ollie knew," my father repeats. "He was worried about me, so he came to join us."

"Worried about you?" I say, disbelieving.

"When someone gets sick, it's hard for everyone in the family. We all have a long road ahead, Will."

"I want to see her," I say. "Right now."

My father looks back toward the glowing lights of the motel. The cheesy, old-fashioned sign out front. He rises, long limbs unfolding, and stands tall. "There must be a way, FaceTime or Skype. Let's stop by the front desk, see if we can figure something out."

My father holds out a hand to pull me up. I feel as light as a feather, as if I could blow away in a breeze. Maybe that's why he holds my hand all the way back to the motel. And maybe it's why, for the first time in years, I don't instantly pull away. I just squeeze tighter.

I don't want to blow away.

Even so, I release his hand when we reach the gravel parking lot.

I've got this.

Ocean in view!
O! The Joy!

—WILLIAM CLARK

CHAPTER FIVE

THE FARAWAY SHORE

I ask to be alone.

I sit at a desk in our plain, bare, wood-paneled motel room. A borrowed laptop sits in front of me.

Like magic, her face appears on the screen.

She looks good, exactly like herself.

"Mom," I say.

"Will!"

She smiles.

My right hand instinctively goes to the computer screen. She swallows and mirrors my movement with her left hand. All five fingertips touch.

"Your father told you," she says.

I nod, watching her.

"I'm sorry," she says. "I didn't know how to say it. *'Hey, I have cancer!'*" She smirks a little at that, makes an exaggeratedly chirpy face, and flashes two thumbs-up.

I have to laugh, despite everything. And my mother laughs, too. Which is good, I guess. We can still laugh. Mom is still Mom.

"I didn't want to tell you this way, over the Internet," she says. "I'm not thrilled with your father about how this was handled."

"It was okay," I say, defending him. "You know Dad."

She shakes her head. "I do, I do." Then her expression changes. "Cancer isn't contagious, Will. You should know that."

"I know," I say sharply.

She pushes away a strand of hair. "Sorry, I'm new at this. All the articles stress that parents are supposed to tell their children that it's not contagious."

I can't think of anything to say. *I'm not five years old*. What does an article know about *me*?

She leans into the camera. Her face looms larger, Oz-like. "This illness . . . this cancer . . . may scare and exhaust me, Will, but it will not kill me."

You don't know that, I think.

"How do you feel?" I ask.

"Okay," she says. "Surprisingly good, actually. They say the first couple of weeks aren't that bad. Aunt Barbara has been here with me. Pampering me. She just dropped everything and came." My mother laughs. "Barbara even brought her healing rocks and massage table—on the plane!"

"Really? That's crazy." My aunt Barbara, my mother's sister, is a massage therapist, something like that, and she's pretty out there.

"She's burning oils for 'healing' and 'tranquility,' making my favorite split pea soup, massaging my feet, doing laundry, driving me to the hospital," she says.

"That's nice," I reply. But I feel envious and fall silent. Perhaps she notices the change in my expression.

"I'm glad you're with your father now," she says. "It's important to me that you two spend time together. But I will be gladder when you're home and I can wrap my arms around you. Will you let me do that, Will? Even though you're becoming a young man?"

She blinks back a tear, trying to act brave. I don't know what it is about tears, but if I see somebody crying—it can be over the stupidest thing, even on a television commercial—then I automatically cry, too. A little bit. I don't feel like such a young man. Just the opposite. So I nod yes, she can hug me all she wants.

"I should be there with you," I say.

"You will be," she answers. "This is going to be a long, long road. I wanted some time to be alone in the beginning, to get my act together. I needed to focus on just me. I'm sorry. It sounds so selfish."

I tell her that I understand, it wasn't selfish at all, though I'm not sure I fully get it. Maybe it's like being on deck in a baseball game. It's that time when a batter has to narrow his focus, study the pitcher, get ready for the coming at bat. Something like that.

She asks if I have any questions.

"Will you lose your hair?"

Yes, she will, she tells me. But it will grow back. "This is all temporary," she insists. "A hard thing that we're just going to have to get through together."

Like crossing the Bitterroots, I think.

Another journey.

We talk some more. I tell her about the trip, but not about the bear. The timing doesn't seem right. I'm ready to get off after she starts asking the typical mother questions: Am I eating well; how's it going with Dad; am I warm enough?

"I love you," she tells me.

"Me too, Mom. I love you, too." Then I remember the thing I forgot. "And, Mom?"

"Yes?"

"We got a dog—and he's really, really big!"

My father pokes his head into the room. "All done?"

"Yeah." I push away from the table. "It was good. She says hi."

"I've got to return the laptop to the main desk," he says, tucking the computer under his arm. "Want to come for a stroll? There's a million stars out tonight."

We drift away from the lights of the motel and onto a quiet road, in order to better see the stars. We are comfortable without words.

"It really must have been something," my father says after a long silence. And I know that he's thinking about the old days, before the white men came to this land. Before there were bright lights and paved highways. He's gazing at the stars, staring up at the miraculous universe. "We can head home tomorrow," he says.

"I'd like to keep going," I reply.

He looks at me, surprised.

"Mom says it's okay."

"All the way?" he asks.

I shrug. "How far is it?"

He rubs his jaw, calculating the route in his mind. I notice that he hasn't shaved in a while. The scruff looks good on him. "Let's see. If we go directly, don't stop along the way—"

"No more museum stops," I say. "I'm full up on Lewis and Clark interpretive centers."

"Well, we'll miss a lot of history. You know that, right?" He starts to tick off the names of places, then catches himself. "I'm sorry, I know you want to get back home to your mom, too. I understand that."

"Can't we just kind of . . . blam through?" I ask.

"Blam? Sure, fair enough," he answers. "In that

case, I think we can make it in nine, ten hours' hard driving."

I'm glad. "I want to reach the ocean, don't you?"

He smiles up at the Idaho night sky. "To the sea!" he shouts, arms up in triumph, fists clenched. "All the way to the sea!"

"You're so weird," I observe.

"Isn't everybody?" he asks, but it's not a question that requires an answer.

Forgot to mention that I almost got eaten by a black bear. Ironic, huh, since I was always worried about the grizzlies. Anyway, that would have sucked, right? Other than that, no worries! I talked it over with Dad, and you were right. We've decided to go all the way to the ocean. Finish this up properly. Then I'm headed home to you, Mom. Love you, xo, Will!

We eat breakfast in the main section of the motel. There's a sign that reads, ANYTHING CAN BE SOLVED OVER A STACK OF PANCAKES.

It's worth a try, right?

I order a side of bacon.

While I happily munch, my father wanders over to talk to some local men. When he sits back down with me, he pores over a map. He lifts his head, and I can tell that he's got something on his mind. His eyes are bright and wild. He says, "There's one last stop I'd like to make, but only if it's okay with you."

"No more museums," I remind him. "I just can't, Dad."

"No, nothing like that," my father says, laughing. "Actually, I think you're going to love this."

"Yeah, and?"

He jabs an index finger on the map. "White-water rapids, Will. One last, heart-pounding adventure. What do you say?"

The Corps of Discovery stayed with the Nez Perce for two weeks. They needed time to recover from their mountain crossing. After surviving almost entirely on meat, the Nez Perce diet of salmon and roots did not agree with the men's bellies.

Many fell extremely ill, including Captain Lewis. They also faced another problem. They needed canoes to navigate the river passage. The men lacked strength and good axes. Fortunately a chief of the Nez Perce, Twisted Hair, taught Captain Clark a new technique for dugout canoes. Near the bank of the Clearwater River, they found ponderosa pines that were wide enough for canoes. The Nez Perce method was to a use a slow, steady fire to burn a trench out of the fallen trees. After ten days of work, Clark and his men had carved five new canoes. Though the water was very fast—and the most dangerous rapids lay ahead—the Corps of Discovery was ready to continue their journey. It was early October, the weather was changing, and they were determined to reach the sea before winter. Thanks to the help of the Nez Perce, once again the Corps was on their way!

"The Columbia was a wild, treacherous river back in the time of Lewis and Clark," my father explains.

"Over the years, engineers for the government built more than a dozen dams and reservoirs to tame the river. It's not like it used to be back when there was nothing to stop the river's flow down from the mountains. That river once carved channels between cliffs that are now three thousand feet high. These days it's . . . *pfftt*."

He tells me that the final part of the journey for the Corps of Discovery was a dangerous run through churning rapids. "Those times are gone, for the most part, but I wanted to give you a sense of their journey, the *spirit* of it. So we're going to backtrack a bit to find a spot here on the Lochsa River"—he pronounces it *lock-saw*—"to get our thrills."

"Wait, really?" I ask. "You always said I was too young."

"You were too young," he replies. "But you've grown up, Will. Normally you'd need to be sixteen years old for these boat trips. But since it's late in the season, we should be okay. The rapids aren't as bad."

"Are you sure?"

He looks at me, head cocked to the side. "No," he says, grinning.

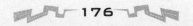

Amazingly, I can almost feel my heart beat in my chest. A swelling that goes: *ba-boom, ba-boom, ba-boom*. I'm excited and nervous for a new adventure.

My father continues, "The local Indians thought these reckless white men were going to get themselves killed, traveling in hard-to-steer dugout canoes. So all along the journey, the Native people lined the riverbanks to watch as the expedition came through. It was great entertainment."

We arrive at the Lochsa Lodge, sign in, and gear up. It's late in the season, we're told. Most of the winter melt has already come down from the mountains, so the river is lower and slower. I'm secretly relieved. We study a huge river map on the wall. The Class III rapids we'll be shooting have names like Pipeline and Grim Reaper. "Sounds promising," my father notes. There are photos of plants and animals we might see: emerald ferns, huckleberries, mountain spray, cedar and fir trees, ospreys, wolves, eagles, even otters. The list goes on. I have time to pick up another postcard and a sweet sweatshirt in the gift shop. Finally, we gather around our boisterous river guide, who introduces himself as "Dan the River Man."

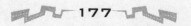

He's a muscular, shaggy-haired, bearded outdoors-man, probably in his early thirties. He assures us that this is not his first rodeo. Our group includes six other adults in addition to my father and me, and we're assigned a big orange inflatable raft. It looks bouncy and safe. We're all dressed in rented wet suits and wear life vests and plastic helmets.

Before we even get into the water, Dan makes a few jokes to show us he's a cool guy, and then shifts into a no-nonsense talk about river safety. We go over a list of dos and don'ts—mostly don'ts. Dan steps up and with a firm yank tightens each individual life vest. Next Dan drills us on paddle techniques. Some of it I already know, thanks to Ollie. We're going to have to work hard and listen to his instructions, when to "dig in" and put our backs into it, when to shift our weight, and when to lie back. "We can't possibly avoid every obstacle on the river. Let's say, oh, we're going to roll over a rock. I'll shout out, 'Bump!' When that happens, you've all got to lean into the center of the boat. It's critically important. We don't want any-body falling over the side." Dan scans the group, and his gaze lingers longest on me, maybe because I'm the youngest. "Mistakes can cost lives," Dan reminds us. And he says to my father, "Make sure you two sit near me."

Dan gives us a final inspection, and we put in at a quiet bend of the river. Soon the water carries us away. It doesn't stay quiet for long.

The first hour is probably the most exciting sixty minutes I've had in my entire life. And then with a lurch the boat suddenly tips down, and there's a bounce and a jostle, and Dan cries out, "Big bump! Lean in!" Before I can react, I'm popped backward into the air like a rag doll. My feet kick at the clouds. The paddle flies from my hands.

I cry out something like, "Aaargggh!" or "Whaaaaaazit!" But mostly it all unreels like a movie, a rapid-fire succession of flickering images across a screen. The only sound is the river's unremitting roar.

I hit the water, and I'm instantly thrown into a frenzied, swirling liquid mass of pure force. I have no control over my body; I'm just tumbling and rolling in the helter-skelter of rapids. It's like getting hit by a locomotive, then another one, then another one. I'm buried under for a horrifying ten seconds, gulping water in a panic, and then I'm thrown up into the light, lungs screaming for air. From the corner of my eye I see the raft ahead of me, shocked faces staring back, my father shouting wordlessly, arms waving, pointing. There's Dan in his silver Ray-Bans, ever cool, standing at the back of the boat. He looks back at me over his shoulder, assessing the situation, while still navigating the course ahead.

I am a bullet, shooting the rapids.

I'm kicking against the water uselessly. My arms windmill. I crash hard against a rock, *oomph*, reach for it with one hand, but the powerful current drags me away. The life vest keeps me afloat while the river plunges me forward. I go under again, shut my mouth, and this time miraculously remember *not* to breathe. My head takes a glancing blow against an outcrop of rocks, but the helmet protects me from the full impact. I'm on the edge of losing it, heart jackhammering, thinking that I'm going to drown here—thinking, *I can't believe I'm going to die so stupidly, so unexpectedly!*—I'm thrashing and lashing out against the current, when suddenly it hits me: a dead calm.

A clarity.

I can't explain it.

I simply remember what I'm supposed to do.

And the first rule, number one, is this:

Stay calm.

The world slows down. I'm in a tunnel, and I know exactly what to do.

"Nose and toes to the sky," Dan told us.

I float on my back, bringing my arms close to my sides. I adjust my course so I'm flowing feet first, legs together. If I brush against an obstacle, my bent knees absorb the shock and with a slight shift I roll to my left or right. In this way, I'm steering in subtle ways, like down the big slide at Water Park World. When I can, I take a deep breath of air; when white water crashes over me, I wait it out, holding my breath.

Occasionally I hear cries and shouted directions. The orange raft is not far away. They will reach me. I just have to do my part.

I merely have to stay alive.

I look up at the sky.

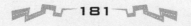

It is the clearest, prettiest blue I've ever seen. Not a cloud in sight. A raptor takes flight, soaring from left to right, and then it's gone, tilting sideways, behind me. A falcon, probably. What did Ollie tell me? *The vision of a great raptor feeds the heart, lifts the soul, gives one courage.* I have to wait this out, stay lucky, and keep floating. In time the force of the water subsides. I close my eyes, bobbing in the water, peaceful.

I know, crazily, in that instant, it's going to be okay. I decide to enjoy the ride.

Something claws at my neck, a hand grabs at my vest, more hands hoist me up and over and into the raft. Shouts of relief fill the air, and there's my dad's face hovering over me, eyes beaming, as happy as I've ever seen him.

I've learned that my father and I talk best when we are walking or driving. When we don't have to look at each other. I don't know why that's so. It feels less trapped, I guess, less like I'm an insect pinned down in some scientist's glass case.

Back in the car, I ask:

"*Will she be okay?*"

We are still headed west, toward the ocean, to a town called Seaside, Oregon.

"Yes," my father answers.

He looks straight ahead. The road curves; traffic merges; he is alert and attentive. Serious business.

"Okay," I say.

I don't believe him.

After a while, he says in a weird, choked whisper, "The truth is, Will, I don't know. No one can truthfully answer that question."

He glances at me. My hands are folded, fingers entwined on my lap. Like a gross pale spider.

"I believe in my heart that your mom will get through this," he says. "And I want you to believe that, too. It's important to think positive thoughts. But I won't lie. It's going to be a difficult road, Will. There will be times when she's going to be very sick. You'll need to be strong and brave and kind."

He reaches out and puts an arm around my shoulders. "I'm not going anywhere, Will. I'll help out as best as I can—even though," he adds, "we're still divorced."

Strong and brave and kind.

I sag a little right then and crumple like a tower of cards from the weight of it, letting my head fall to his lap. In that instant, I am a little boy again, afraid of the dark. I look straight ahead, watching his feet work the pedals, and promise myself, "I will be."

Strong and brave and kind.

But not yet, not this minute.

Right now I just want to be a kid.

My father slides down his window. "Can you smell it, Will?"

I sit up, rubbing my eyes. The air feels fresh. Cool and clear. There's a scent to it that I don't immediately recognize. Then it hits me. "Salt?"

"We're almost there."

The end of the trail.

Seaside is a beach town, with a long boardwalk, high buildings off the shore, and a stunning sand beach. It's late in the afternoon, and most of the traffic is heading the other way—leaving, not

arriving. There's a traffic turnaround with a giant statue looming in the center. My father pulls over by the curb. We step out, stiff legged, and look to the ocean. There it is, waiting for us. There's an island to our left in the shape of a green, tree-lined pyramid. I turn to check out the bronze statue behind us. It's Lewis and Clark again, at least fifteen feet tall, standing on a big round base, facing the ocean. A wooden sign that's as tall as my father reads:

SEASIDE OREGON
THE END OF THE LEWIS & CLARK TRAIL
1805-1806

We cross to inspect the statue more closely. They stand on a pile of rocks and driftwood, and at their feet is a dog. I point up. "It looks just like Paco."

"That was Meriwether's dog, Seaman," he explains. "He made the trip, too."

"A Newfoundland?" I ask.

My father nods, smiling at the coincidence.

"It took them four thousand miles and eighteen months to get here," my father muses.

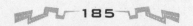

"It took us less than two weeks," I say.

My father cranes his neck, looking up and down the shore. "A few soldiers came here and built a salt-making cairn. There's a pretty cool living museum right around here someplace . . ."

I give him *the look*.

"Okay, okay," he says. "Sometimes I can't help myself."

I notice there's no one swimming in the ocean. "How cold is it?" I wonder.

We cross to the car. My father pulls out two large towels. "Below sixty, for sure. Actually, it's warmer here than anywhere else in Oregon, because of the influence of the Columbia River. People generally don't swim in it unless they're wearing a wet suit."

"We came all this way. Gotta do it," I say.

My father pulls off his shirt, shoes, and socks. His pants come next. He stands in his orange boxers, a light rain in the air. He's that rare thing, a skinny dad. "It's going to be cold," he warns.

I stand shivering on the water's edge in basketball shorts. I am already cold. I think of our trip, the long journey we've taken to arrive at this place. Here on

the far western shore, the knife edge of America. And I think of my mother, maybe getting treatment in a hospital at this very moment, an IV drip attached to her arm, the medicine flowing into her body. *She's going to feel very, very sick.* My mother is on a journey of her own. But she will not be alone. I am coming home.

"Come on," I say to my father.

He hesitates, frowning at the gray ocean. "During the winter, a great whale beached up when they were wintering at Fort Clatsop, not too far from here. Even Sacagawea traveled to see it. She had never seen the ocean before."

He's stalling, I realize.

"Come on," I urge.

"I don't know," he says. "You go. I'll wait here with the towels."

No way. We have to do this together. I look at him, and he knows it's true. He can't squirm out of this. Some things just have to be endured. He gives me a shove, discards the towels, and the next moment we are running hard into the Pacific.

At the instant my first step reaches the water, I feel

a bolt of ice-cold surge up my body. But I'm moving too fast; there's no turning back now. And then I'm laughing—we're both howling and screaming and yelping in shock and surprise—splashing and shivering.

I dive into the ocean and come up laughing. It isn't so bad, I lie to myself, standing hip deep in the water. My father's lips are already turning blue. We high-five, happy and a little wired, and we hurry back to shore.

It's time to try to get warm again.

"You know, we're not far from Seattle," my father says.

We're on the promenade, dusting the sand off our feet, pulling on our socks over still-numb toes.

"And?"

"And I've never taken you to a professional baseball game," he says. "I'm not proud of that. I looked it up earlier today. The Mariners are home. If we stay one more day, I was thinking that maybe—"

"No," I cut him off. "I mean, that would be amazing. I'd love to go to a real game someday." I pause,

glancing toward the Pacific. "I just want to get back home."

He claws at his hair with both hands and complains, "Stupid sand gets everywhere."

I wait, watching him. "Besides, I want to see the Twins in the Metrodome."

He looks at me like it was the first time it had ever occurred to him. "We can do that," he says, reaching out a hand.

I take it and shake on it.

Deal.

"It was dumb idea anyway," he admits. "Staying an extra night, driving up to Seattle. My credit card bill is going to go kablooey. I guess I don't want our trip to end."

It's a strange moment for me, because I feel like we've been switched. I'm the grown-up, and he's the kid. My father might be more afraid of going back than I am. Hard times ahead.

I stand and stretch, look toward the car. I point to it, the clear path.

He accepts the hint. "You ready to go home?"

"How far is it?" I ask.

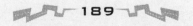

"Almost two thousand miles." He rubs both eyes with his long fingers. "Probably thirteen hours back to Dillon—"

"—and Maria and Paco," I say, finishing his sentence. We climb into the car.

"We can crash near there," he says. "Arrange to pick up Paco in the morning. Then it's about another sixteen, eighteen hours to Minneapolis. Depends on how often we stop. I'll coffee up and try to power straight through."

"Are you sure you'll be okay?"

"Will," he says, placing a hand on my shoulder, "I've got you."

The key goes into the ignition.

"You ready?"

I am, yes. I am so ready.

I realized today that I hadn't thought about baseball until Dad brought it up. Isn't that bizarre? I hope my All-Star team is doing well without me—but not too well! Ha-ha! There is one thing I do think about every

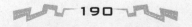

day, and that's you. Home before you know it, probably before you even get this card! xo, Will

"Hello, hello!" Maria Rosa calls down from the top of the stairs. She stands in the second-floor hallway of her apartment building, waving us up. Paco wags his tail, gives a short friendly yip, and smiles the way dogs sometimes do.

"Hey, Paco! You remember me," I say, taking his big black head in my hands.

"Come in, *por favor*," Maria says. She tucks a strand of hair behind an ear and smiles.

"English, Maria," Alejandro chides from the doorway.

She blushes, then brightens. "Please, please, please, come see my new home! Happy now, Alejandro?"

Everyone laughs.

She admits, "I watch so much television. I like *The Price Is Right* very much. It helps with my English. Alejandro says"—she glances to her cousin—"that it is *importante* for me to . . . *hablar inglés.*"

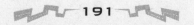

She flashes a teasing smile at Alejandro. He taps a palm against his forehead, shaking it as if in misery, and laughs.

Alejandro sweeps his arm, gesturing for us to come inside. "Please," he says, grinning.

We gather around a small kitchen table. Alejandro wears jeans and a T-shirt, with the same red bandana from last week hanging from a belt loop. There are grease stains on his pants, but his fingernails, I notice, are immaculate. There are only three chairs, and he insists that we take them. I see how he holds the chair out for Maria Rosa. With an athletic turn, he hoists himself up to the kitchen countertop where he sits, sockless, feet dangling. He seems perfectly relaxed. It's hard to explain. He's softer than when we first met him. More relaxed and at home. I guess we gave him a shock that day at the gas station. Or maybe it is Maria Rosa who has softened his heart.

My father accepts Maria's offer of coffee, which she sets before him. I ask for water, no ice. I'm forced to explain to Alejandro that I hate ice, that I think it's totally useless, which somehow comes as news to my father.

"I've never heard of such a thing," he says.

"Dad, I've always hated ice."

Oh well. A lot of things float over his head. I suppose they always will.

The apartment is cozy, filled with random furniture. It is also spotless. Maria's touch, perhaps, but I'm not sure.

"So," my father announces, as if he'd offered a complete thought. He pauses, looks from Alejandro to Maria. "How are you two getting along?"

"*Bueno*," Maria says, instantly recognizing her mistake. "Very good."

"Have you seen a doctor?" my father asks.

Alejandro speaks up. "There is a clinic. I plan to take her on Wednesday. It is a long drive," he explains. Maria listens, nodding, absently running a hand across her belly. It's easy for me to forget that there's a child in there, waiting.

While they talk, I sink to the floor with Paco. The dog lounges in a patch of morning sunlight. He's just the sort of dog I've always wanted. The wrestle-around-with-me type. Big and gentle. My friend Yoenis has a dog, a lively mutt. Maybe we'll be able to bring our dogs to the park together. Maybe they will be friends. I can't believe he's mine. My first dog. Or he will be, very soon, when we leave. I try not to think about how this must feel for Maria Rosa.

Soon the kitchen conversation runs out of words. My father writes something down on a piece of paper, folds it, and passes it across to Maria. "That's my number and e-mail address if you ever need anything—they have free computers you can use at the public library." He rises, rinses his cup in the sink. "So," he says again. "We have a long ride ahead of us." He stretches in a backward arc, arms wide, face to the ceiling. Maria looks to Paco. She blinks. Her lips turn into a thoughtful pout. She knows what's going to happen next. Alejandro seems to notice. He pops down off the counter to stand beside her. "It's better," he says softly, and she nods, as if she almost believes it.

My father wanders over to a small bookshelf across the living room. It's built with cinder blocks and two-by-fours. He runs a finger across the book spines, murmuring in approval. He pulls out a book and holds it up to Alejandro. "Borges," he says. "You've read it?"

Alejandro nods, yes.

"Amazing writer," my father says.

"He is difficult for me," Alejandro says, stepping closer. "Each story is simple, and yet . . . a wonder." He joins my father by the books. I am glad to see this, for books—I see again—are the way into my father's heart.

Watching them talk, I remember an experiment we did in elementary school on electricity. We were studying conductors and insulators. There was a battery, wire, alligator clips, and a lightbulb. The idea was to test which materials conducted electricity. We tried a bunch of things—wood, rubber bands, string, plastic, paper clips, marshmallows—you name it. When it comes to finding a way to get my dad to light up, books are the best conductors.

Maybe I need to read more books. Or maybe we can read a book together, like we used to when I was little. Is that too babyish? I hope not.

Maria Rosa kneels beside me. She places a hand on Paco's back. The dog looks up at her, wondering. If they speak, it is not in words. She finally whispers, "It's better, Paco. You'll see."

It is hard to watch the tears rolls down her face. I look away. When I look back, she has smeared them into her cheeks, so that her face shines. She works up a smile for me, but her eyes tell a different story.

"Ah, I forgot your present!" I exclaim, jumping to my feet.

I have to run back to the car to get it. When I return, breathless, my father already has Paco by the leash. He's holding a blanket tucked under his arm.

"I didn't have time to wrap it," I say, handing Maria the gift. "Do you know what it is?"

"A dream catcher," she says.

"I bought it at a stop on the side of the road," I say, suddenly filled with doubt. "Maybe it's stupid, I don't know."

"No, no," Maria says. "I have so many dreams."

"Really?" I say. "Because that's what I thought, you know, that maybe you have dreams and

hopes . . ." I run out of gas, like a car stalled on the highway, no longer sure of what I'm trying to say.

I don't know what else to say. There are no words for this. Except, I guess, good-bye.

She opens her arms, gathers me into her embrace. "Sweet boy," she says. "Be good to my Paco."

They walk us out the door into the bright morning light. "Thank you," Maria Rosa says over and over again. "You saved me. Thank you, thank you."

At last, Alejandro cups a hand around his mouth. "She means *gracias*!" he shouts.

They are still laughing as we drive away.

Sure beats crying.

Paco sleeps on the backseat, comfortable on his old blanket. On the drowsy night road, under the slashing streaks of highway lights, my thoughts return to my mother. I ask my father if it helps to pray.

"It can't hurt," he offers.

"But does it work?"

My father takes a deep breath, blows it out. This

is how he stalls while he tries to decide if I should hear the truth.

I am old enough, I think. *Just tell me.*

He says, "I believe there are people who are very good, who pray often and try each day to serve their god, but still tragedy befalls them. Their prayers seem to go unanswered. And then there are terrible people, selfish and small-minded, and somehow they seem to skate free." He pauses, wipes his face. "I don't know how it works, Will. No idea. I truly wish I did. I'm sorry, it's the best answer I can give."

I decide to pray.

Actually, I don't *decide* it. There's no decision. Prayer just sort of happens. The thoughts well up inside me, like a cup overflowing, rising up from my belly, as if I'm answering a call from heaven. *Dear God*, I whisper inside my head, *please, dear God . . .*

My father listens to the radio. Scratchy voices talking about guns and war. I turn it off. "Dad, I've been thinking about that bear."

"Oh?" he says.

"That was very possibly the worst throw I have ever seen in my entire life."

We both laugh about that, we just laugh and laugh.

It was a long trip. For Lewis and Clark—and for my dad and me, too. They weren't perfect, those men. It was a long time ago. They made mistakes. It's sad to think about what happened to the great Indian tribes who had never seen a white man before Lewis and Clark arrived. For the Native people of America, it was the beginning of a long chain of broken promises and suffering.

Lewis and Clark's journey was, I think, maybe one of the greatest adventures that ever happened in America. The ultimate camping trip. It was also a story of cruelty and of the horrible way that "progress" rolled over everything in its path. After the Corps of Discovery, young men and women went west in wave after wave after wave. They built houses, fences,

roads, railroad tracks. They cleared forests and built dams and tamed rivers. The land would never be wild again. But there are places where I could still feel the old, "weird" America— standing at the Lemhi Pass or watching an eagle soar in the wind by the White Cliffs or just staring in wonder at the Pacific Ocean. Those are the feelings I will keep in my heart.

Even as we tried to retrace their footsteps, new things got in our way. There was the Nez Perce Indian named Ollie, and the pregnant girl, Maria Rosa, the black bear and eagle, and my splash into the raging Lochsa River. Along the way I began to understand that it wasn't necessary to follow the trail perfectly. It was the spirit of the thing that mattered: exploring new places, meeting new people, facing new challenges. We went out to discover a piece of history, and maybe learn about America, but I think we came back with something more. I know I'll never look at an eagle the same way again. My father and I shared time together, and we're better now. Not

*perfect, but better. I feel ready to face what's next,
even my mom's cancer. There will be tough times
ahead. Captain Lewis knew it. But he went forward anyway. That's the spirit I want to live
by—the courage to keep going.*

*So, yeah, that's what I did my summer
vacation!*

"Lewis and Clark returned as conquering heroes," my
father says. "People came out to greet them. To clap
and cheer. Remember, a lot of these folks figured
they'd never see those men again." He makes a gesture of a finger slicing across his throat. "Maybe you'll
get some of that when you get home."

"Yoenis will be glad to see me," I say.

"Yoenis? That's some name."

"He moved here recently from Cuba," I say. "A
good baseball and soccer player, but he hates hockey."

My father whistles. "A Cuban in Minnesota who
hates hockey, that's rough."

"He can't skate," I explain.

"You could teach him."

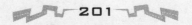

"Maybe," I say.

"Next time maybe we can bring him along," he says.

"Hey," I say. "Do you really mean it about a *next time?*"

He looks at me sideways, assessing my meaning. "If you want to," he says. "There's so much we didn't see. Lewis was gone for two and half years. We took about two weeks."

"Yeah, where would you want to go next time?" I ask, and settle in for a lengthy answer.

My father talks and talks, warming to his favorite topic. He names places and recounts adventures on the trail. All the things we could do in the future.

"Do you think Mom could come?" I ask. And I can tell by the way his face changes that I have hoped for too much. My same old mistake. His mouth opens, shuts. After a sigh, he says, "It's possible, maybe, you never know."

"She would like this," I say.

"I know she's glad we did it," he says.

"Me too," I say.

I didn't know what else to say. I remember there

was a time when we were together, my father, my mother, and me. A time that I know is lost forever.

"She was different in those days," my father murmurs, filling the silence. "I guess we all were."

Time passes. Autumn comes and goes, now winter lingers. We don't mess around when it comes to winter here in Minneapolis, Minnesota. We're all in. Winter is the houseguest that settles in like a big dog in front of a crackling fire.

My mom's in the kitchen, fixing dinner. Paco's in there with her, of course, because he follows her around nearly everywhere, especially when she's cooking. I think my mother sneaks him treats. She's softhearted that way. I'm glad we have a dog, even though it means extra vacuum duty for me. My mom jokes that Paco is just a big, dumb, slobbery love machine—but I don't think he's dumb at all. The slobber and the love? Well, she's right about that. She saved all my postcards from the trail, and now every single one is taped neatly to our fridge. Every day I'm reminded of those two weeks with my father—the bear and the river and diving into that cold, cold ocean. I want to go back someday, retrace those steps, and visit new places, too.

I guess Mom has good days and not-so-good days, but more good than bad. So far, so good. Her hair is starting to grow back. It doesn't look the same as it used to; it's not as soft as before, but she says it'll come around, give it time. I don't know. To be honest, I liked her wigs better. She even wore a hot pink one every once in a while. Mom says it's her way of giving the middle finger to cancer. We still laugh, maybe more than ever.

Dad comes by every week. Wednesday night dinners, the three of us. The new normal. Instead of taking me to Angela's restaurant, he brings takeout for all three of us, maybe crawls under the sink to fix a leak, that kind of thing. I can see that he's trying to be a good man.

We get postcards from Maria Rosa. She's like me that way. We like the pictures. Maria had her baby. A girl, only four pounds, nine ounces. Little Daniela. Dad jokes that it's good she didn't have a boy, or else she might have named him Paco, which might have upset our dog. Maria worked for a while, help-ing care for an older lady, but now she's mostly tak-ing care of the baby. She signed up for night classes. Maria's dream is to become a nurse. I wonder if she snagged that in her dream catcher.

"She has big plans, that one," my father observes.

"I know," I say.

I hope they come true.

My mother still wears the bracelet that I bought from Maria back at Fort Benton. I see it on her wrist every day. It makes me happy. It connects them, Maria and my mother, even though they've never met. Late at night sometimes I awake in the solid dark, remembering her. Oh, and it turns out that Maria's cousin Alejandro is a writer. He e-mails my father every once in a while and includes short sto-ries and poems. My father says they are very good. He might even get published. Isn't that something?

For the most part, I've kept the promise I made to myself. I try to be strong and brave and kind. I believe my mother's going to be all right. And I still lie back in bed each night, my head on the pillow. I squeeze my eyes tight so I see a swirl of dancing colors, and I pray.

I send my hopes and wishes out into the universe like a scattering of stars in the night sky. *I wish I may, I wish I might.*

I remember how it began. That day she pushed me out the door into my father's arms, as if she needed for us to be together. *He's the only father you've got,* she said. So out we went, headed west. To close our wounds, to open our hearts, to prepare for the courage test ahead. Someday, maybe today, it's a story I'll try to put into words.

After we got back, I had to tackle my summer assignment. Normally I'd wait until the last days of summer, but not this time. I started writing right away.

My name is William Meriwether Miller. I was named after the explorers William Clark and Meriwether Lewis. It was my dad's idea. So I guess this trip was inevitable. . . .

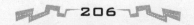

AUTHOR'S NOTE

At the beginning, this book was inspired by Roald Dahl's *Danny the Champion of the World*. I came to Dahl's classic late, and I was struck by the strong father-son element that provided the backbone of the story. Somehow, this book gave me license to consider writing my own father-son story, a dynamic I don't often see in middle-grade fiction.

I decided on a journey, a road trip along—why not?—the westward part of the old Lewis and Clark Trail. At that initial stage, Lewis and Clark's famous journey served merely as metaphor. I didn't know a whole lot about it. My starting point was simple. In preparation for coming hardships, Will's father is determined to drag his reluctant son halfway across the country in the footsteps of Lewis and Clark. He seeks to teach his son the life lessons of their curiosity, resourcefulness, and undaunted courage. And that maybe, somehow, this trip would serve to strengthen their bond. I even had an image of a late scene for the book: the father with his key in the ignition, the car pointed back east, asking his son, "You ready?" The idea, I hoped, would be that yes, now he was ready.

That's when I began the real research, getting deeper into the historic record. The more I learned, the more fascinated I became and the more I wanted to share. I'd accidentally hit upon a rich pathway into the American soul. The scope of the book shifted under me. The Trail was no longer merely metaphor; it became essential fact. So now, here we are, and this book has become an expression of my awe and wonder at the exploration made by Lewis and Clark from 1804–06. Theirs was a bold journey into unmapped territory, revealing sights never before held by white men—the first epic and fateful push west that came to define the American pioneering impulse. It is a story of discovery and nation-making, of bravery and perseverance.

Most profoundly, the exploration included a tragic clash of cultures between American settlers—who believed that the United States government had purchased the land—and the Native people who had already lived there for centuries.

And so, I set a father and son wandering along that same path, some two hundred years later, to discover America. In the process, they learn something of themselves, certainly, but also this: that we are forever remaking this great nation in a thousand different ways. How we respect the land, how we treat each other. Each day, we define ourselves anew. This was our history, our story, all of us, even those new immigrants who are yet to arrive.

To the best of my ability and within the context of the book's semi-reliable narrator (Will is not an expert), the historic information presented in this book is accurate. While I made use of a wide variety of books and Internet resources, I owe the greatest debt to *Undaunted Courage* by Stephen E. Ambrose, *The Journals of Lewis Clark* edited by Bernard DeVoto, *Lewis and Clark Through Indian Eyes: Nine Indian Writers on the Legacy of the Expedition* edited by Alvin M. Josephy Jr., *Lewis and Clark Among the Indians* by James P. Ronda, and *Traveling the Lewis and Clark Trail* by Julie Fanselow. A documentary by Ken Burns, *Lewis & Clark: The Journey of the Corps of Discovery*, was both informative and entertaining; there is also a fine companion book of the same title. A simple Internet search will yield dozens of excellent sites for the traveler interested in following in the footsteps of the Lewis and Clark Trail.

However, I do wish to clarify a few things:

York, a slave—a man owned as the property of William Clark—eventually did earn his freedom, though it took at least ten years after the expedition's triumphant return before Clark freed him. The historic record is incomplete and conflicting, as if York was a man little worth noting. One legend has York returning to upper Missouri as a free man, going off to live with a tribe of Crow. However, most historians believe that York contracted cholera and died somewhere in Tennessee after working in the trade industry. The exact date and location of his death remains unknown. In many ways, York's stunted life serves to illuminate the tragic, cruel legacy of slavery in America.

Despite facing countless hazards along the way, only one member of the original expedition died on the trip. His name was Charles Floyd, a sergeant who fell sick of an unknown stomach ailment that modern doctors now believe was an infected appendix. He died on August 20, 1804, and was buried on a bluff close to present-day Sioux City, Iowa. A monument now marks the spot.

While the journey was generally remarkable in its nonviolence and for the spirit of cooperation in the expedition's encounters with the Native people, there were dangerous encounters along the way. Most notably, serious violence fueled by deep mutual distrust (guns and bows were raised) almost erupted during a visit with the Sioux in South Dakota.

On a later occasion, shots were fired during a fierce struggle with a small group of Blackfeet near the Marias River in northern Montana, resulting in the death of at least one Native person with another victim likely, but unconfirmed. The sections of the trail where these conflicts occurred were not retraced by Will and his father, and therefore did not fall within the realm of this book.

Thanks largely to the considerable skills of Meriwether Lewis, the expedition recorded an estimated 180 plants and 120 animals not previously known to science. Some animals include: the mountain lion, coyote, wolverine, elk, prairie dog, mountain goat, golden eagle, whooping crane, and horned lizard. Snakeweed, bearberry, ponderosa pine, bitterroot (Montana's state flower), cottonwood, wild onion, and prickly pear compose just a small sampling of the plants first observed and noted in scientific detail over the course of the expedition.

The proper spelling of Sacagawea is still debated among scholars. Today, her name can be found spelled as Sacagawea, Sakakawea (widely adopted in North Dakota), or Sacajawea (most frequently found in Idaho). Sacagawea is the spelling most widely accepted by scholars, and is also endorsed by the U.S. Board on Geographic Names.

Lewis bought a large, black Newfoundland while preparing for the expedition in Pittsburgh shortly before setting out

for St. Louis and the exploration proper. The dog, which Lewis named Seaman, made it all the way to the Pacific and back. Seaman served as a valuable watchdog at night against bears, roaming buffalo herds, and other dangers.

The Corps of Discovery were the first white people that the Nez Perce ever encountered. Within the tribe, there was lively debate about how to receive these new visitors. Some argued that these strangers were dangerous and should be killed. However, the Nez Perce acted as gracious hosts to the Corps, welcoming them into their camp, feeding and caring for the weary travelers. It is beyond sad to note that a mere seventy-two years later, the Nez Perce were driven off their sacred land forever by the U.S. military, resulting in a 1,800-mile fighting retreat from their homeland in Oregon to their ultimate capture in Montana less than fifty miles from the Canadian border. This is the story that Ollie tells Will during their time on the river. Sometimes, the history of America—and the indifferent wheel of "progress"—reads like a sad, cruel story.

At the time of this book's writing, there really was a Dairy Queen in Dillon, Montana, and a Denny's in Bismarck, North Dakota. I didn't make that up. Likewise, the statue of faithful Shep that Will saw in Fort Benton, Montana, is still there—and the dog's legend continues to grow. This is true for any other landmarks mentioned in these pages.